First American Edition 2020
Kane Miller, A Division of EDC Publishing

Text © Alesha Dixon, 2018
Cover design by Kat Godard, Dradog
Cover characters and inside illustrations by James Lancett
represented by the Bright Agency © Scholastic, 2018
The right of Alesha Dixon to be identified as
the author of this Work has been asserted by her.

First published in the UK by Scholastic Ltd., 2018
This edition published under license from Scholastic Ltd.

For information contact:
Kane Miller, A Division of EDC Publishing
PO Box 470663
Tulsa, OK 74147-0663
www.kanemiller.com
www.usbornebooksandmore.com
www.edcpub.com

Library of Congress Control Number: 2019946973
Printed and bound in the United States of America
2 3 4 5 6 7 8 9 10
ISBN: 978-1-68464-078-2

ALESHA DIXON

In collaboration with Katy Birchall
Illustrated by James Lancett

Kane Miller
A DIVISION OF EDC PUBLISHING

For my very own little superhero Azura,
the brightest spark of all and the light
of my life!

No one ever warned me that when you get angry, bright sparks might explode from your fingertips.

But that's exactly what happened. One minute I was watching some school bullies round on my little sister on the playground, and the next minute my hands went all hot and tingly and suddenly these beams of light came flying out from my palms, like a lightning storm.

I think I scared myself more than anyone

else. No one actually saw where the sparks came from, just a flash of blinding light behind them, and then when they turned around, there I was staring wide-eyed at my hands and madly wiggling my fingers.

One of the girls snorted as she watched me bring my hand right up to my face, so it was almost touching the end of my nose, and examine my little finger closely.

"Isn't that your older sister, Clara?" she sneered. "What on earth is she *doing*?"

"She's as odd as you are!" sniggered another one, as they all looked me up and down. I gulped.

Getting them to pick on me instead of Clara wasn't *technically* my original plan. I figured I would just tell them to leave her alone, rather than distract them by becoming a human firework. Still, they weren't interested in Clara anymore and it seemed that they weren't all that curious about a random and inexplicable burst of light in the middle of the playground either.

So that was something.

"What do you want, Aurora?" a tall boy said to me, raising his eyebrows.

"U-um..." I stammered, my hands still held up in front of my face. "I was just, uh, looking at my ... scar."

I held out my left hand, so they could see the swirled scar across my palm.

"I was born with it. Weird, isn't it? Scars appear when the skin tissue heals over a wound to protect and strengthen it. Interesting. Right?"

3

This was not my proudest moment.

Clara looked at me as though I had lost my mind. I tried to think of something else to say, something a bit more impressive than healing-skin-tissue facts, but I was still a bit in shock from shooting light beams out of my hands. It had never happened before. The ringleaders glanced at each other in confusion. The tall one opened his mouth to speak, but luckily the bell rang sharply, signaling that break time was over.

"Saved by the bell! Come on, Clara. See you lot later – fun talking to you!" I laughed nervously, as Clara darted round them to stand next to me. I threw my arm round her and hurriedly dragged her toward the school building before they could say anything else.

Kizzy found it hilarious. I decided not to tell her about the whole sparks-coming-out-of-my-hands thing because I didn't want her thinking that her best friend was weird, but I needn't have worried. She knew I was weird.

"Healing skin tissue?" she giggled, getting her favorite pen out from her pencil case and opening her notebook as we waited for Mrs. Damsel to start our health class.

"It was the first thing I could think of," I sighed, looking accusingly at my palm as though it was my scar's fault that I'd said something so silly. "They'll never let me live it down. I think one of them is in gymnastics club with Suzie Bravo, so I bet they'll tell her all about it."

Kizzy and I glanced across to where Suzie was sitting with Georgie Taylor. Georgie was showing Suzie her cool new backpack, which was black and covered in all these small neon flowers. I just knew it was the latest must-have accessory. Georgie was the trendiest person in our year, maybe even in the entire school,

thanks to her mum who was in charge of publicity for loads of big brands, designers and celebrities. Georgie was always getting freebies and she was very creative with her style. I could hear her telling Suzie that she'd stitched on the flowers herself.

I once tried to sew a swimming badge onto my school blazer and somehow managed to sew the sweater I was wearing at the time to the blazer sleeve. I ripped the sweater *and* the blazer when I tried to detach myself.

Fashion is not my strong point.

"Well, who cares what Suzie Bravo

thinks?" Kizzy said sternly, as she swept her light-brown hair back into a smooth ponytail. "Clara is lucky to have a sister like you to stand up for her. It was very brave of you to face those bullies. I wouldn't have been able to do it."

I smiled. This was, of course, a lie. Kizzy is the nicest person in the world and I would know because we've been best friends forever. She lives on the same road as me and we've been "joined at the hip" (as my dad says) since our first day at school. We're both quite shy so it makes sense to just quietly stick together, while people like Suzie Bravo enjoy being the center of attention.

But just because she's shy and petite — one of the shortest girls in our year, in fact — it doesn't mean Kizzy isn't brave enough to stand up to bullies. At the beginning of term, I accidentally kicked a ball at Mr. Mercury, our grumpy new science teacher, and it bounced right off his big bald head. As he turned around slowly with this fierce expression on his face to see who the culprit was, Kizzy stepped forward to apologize. I tried to protest, but she told me very sternly to be quiet. And because she's the nicest person in the world, Mr. Mercury just told her to be more careful in the future and that was that. He even *laughed*. That's the power Kizzy has over people. She can make the grumpiest science teacher on the planet laugh.

Later, she told me she took the blame because I'd already had a bad start with Mr. Mercury. The week of the ball

incident, I had been shaking my pen to get it to work and accidentally flicked blue ink all over his crisp white shirt. She didn't want me to get into even more trouble.

If that's not bravery, I don't know what is.

As Mrs. Damsel told us all to quiet down for the beginning of class, I tried to forget about my lame scar conversation and instead focus on the weirdness that had come shooting from my hands on the playground, and whether that was normal or not. I couldn't recall anyone else in our year sparking lightning at their classmates, but maybe it was just part of growing up and I was ahead of everyone else. Mum did say recently that I was looking taller, so maybe it was growing pains or something?

Mrs. Damsel announced that in today's lesson we would be learning about nutrition, and began to write on the whiteboard. Fred Pepe let out a very loud burp, making the class

erupt into giggles. I saw Suzie and Georgie roll their eyes dramatically. Fred was always causing trouble.

"Well, Fred," Mrs. Damsel chuckled, turning back to the class, "that may have been an unusual introduction, but actually it's rather on-topic." She pointed to the whiteboard on which she'd written FOOD in large capital letters. "Does anyone know why Fred burped?"

"Because he's *gross*," Suzie said, flicking her

long, blond hair behind her shoulders. Fred stuck his tongue out at her.

"Because he had extra gas," someone squealed from the back of class, which made everyone explode into uncontrollable laughter.

As Mrs. Damsel attempted to get the class back on track, I got out my phone and, under my desk, sneakily tried to search online for anything about electricity coming out of your fingertips and energy rays shooting out of your hands, but nothing came up except for articles about various comic superheroes who can create light or summon lightning and stuff, which wasn't very helpful.

Fred was now blowing raspberries whenever Mrs. Damsel began talking, and just as she began to threaten him with detention if he didn't stop, I shot my hand up in the air.

"Yes, Aurora?" Mrs. Damsel sighed.

"It's nothing to do with food, but I was

wondering if you could tell us about growing pains?"

"Growing pains?"

"Yes." I took a deep breath. "Is there anything weird that we should be aware of? Anything ... strange that happens?"

I could see Kizzy watching me curiously and I tried to look as innocent as possible, as though the question had just popped randomly into my brain. Mrs. Damsel seemed surprised at the change of topic, but didn't seem too unhappy to move away from the subject of gas. Fred was now distracted by a spider on the windowsill anyway, and Mrs. Damsel smiled with relief as the classroom quieted down again.

"What an interesting question, Aurora, albeit a little off-topic. Yes, now that you're soon turning twelve, some of you may be experiencing growing pains and that can mean your muscles get sore, usually in the legs and around joints."

"That's it?" I asked. "Just ... pains? Nothing else?"

"Hello?" Suzie piped up impatiently. "Why do you think they're called growing *pains*? Now, can we get back to food? I actually have a relevant and interesting question, unlike *some* people." She shot me a pointed look and my face grew hot with embarrassment. "Mrs. Damsel, what is the best nutrition advice you can give to champion gymnasts?"

When the lesson finished and we made our way to our next class, Kizzy remarked that I was being very quiet.

"No, I'm not," I replied, even though I hadn't said a word since my growing pains question.

Mrs. Damsel's control over the class hadn't lasted very long thanks to Fred, who had sneaked up behind Suzie when Mrs. Damsel's back was turned and held the spider he'd

caught from the
windowsill right
in front of Suzie's
face. She had
screamed and jumped

up, knocking over her stool, before Fred had begun chasing her around the room with the spider cupped in his hands.

"The poor spider," Kizzy remarked. "I'm glad Mrs. Damsel made Fred take it outside to the grass. Suzie's screams must have frightened the poor thing. She almost made my eardrums burst."

I nodded in agreement and Kizzy gave me a look.

"Are you *sure* you're all right?" she asked for what must have been the hundredth time.

"Absolutely. I'm great," I lied.

"You're lying," Kizzy said with a knowing smile.

"I am not lying."

"Yes, you are. When you lie, your voice goes very high-pitched. Like a dog whistle."

"It does not!" I squeaked. Kizzy raised her eyebrows victoriously.

I coughed, clearing my throat. "It does not," I repeated in more of a growl.

"OK, well, if you want to talk, you know you can tell me anything," she said.

I nodded, but there was no way I could tell her about what happened on the playground. Not until I knew the answer myself.

Because if suddenly shooting light beams from your hands when you see your little sister getting bullied wasn't growing pains, then what was it?

And why in the world had it happened to me?

Z

As soon as Dad's car pulled into the school driveway to pick us up after school, I could see that he had not had a good day.

His face was all scrunched up behind the wheel and as the car came jolting to a stop in front of us, I could see the weird twitch

in his jaw that he gets whenever Mum does something that bugs him. Like when she turns up the heating full blast but then leaves every window in the house wide open all day. Or that time she insisted on letting her amateur magician friend, Sally, perform at my birthday party against Dad's advice, and then all Sally's white doves got loose and pooped everywhere around the house and we couldn't catch any of them, so Dad had to call up a wildlife removal professional to come herd them.

When one of the doves pooped right in the middle of Dad's head as he frantically ran around trying to catch them, Mum said, "Oh look, Henry, that's good luck!" in this very cheery tone.

That's when I first noticed his signature angry-jaw twitch.

"Where's Alexis?" I asked, climbing into the back seat of the car after Clara, purposefully leaving the front seat for my older brother. I knew better than to try and get in there before him.

"He's already at home," Dad grumbled, staring straight ahead and turning on the ignition.

Clara and I exchanged a confused glance. Alexis was a few years older than me but went to the same school as us, so it made no sense that he would already be at home. We always get collected together.

Unless. . .

"What did he do this time?" Clara asked gleefully.

"Don't ask." Dad sighed. "So, how were your days?"

I considered telling him about the bullies picking on Clara and the weird sparks-flying-out-from-my-fingers thing, but then thought it might be wise to wait until he was in a better mood. Clara stayed quiet too, so she clearly agreed. I had asked her if she was OK while we'd been waiting for Dad to arrive and made her promise to tell me if those bullies ever had a go at her again.

"I don't think they will anymore," she had said with a hint of a smile. "They think you're way weirder than me now."

As soon as we got home, I dropped my bag in the hall and ran upstairs to try to get to Alexis before Dad could stop me. I burst through his bedroom door, slightly out of breath, and found him lying on his bed reading a comic book with his new state-of-the-art headphones on.

"What did you do?" I asked eagerly from the doorway, as Clara ran in behind me.

"Never heard of knocking?" Alexis asked drily, taking off his headphones.

"Come on, tell us what happened."

Alexis couldn't help but smirk. He was always pushing teachers' buttons, and if he had been sent home early from school that meant he'd done something extra creative. Once he programmed the school sound system to blast out hip-hop all day long through the speakers in every classroom and corridor. It took Mrs. Prime, the headmistress, two days to find someone who could fix it. In the meantime, Alexis gained legendary status throughout the school.

"I hacked into the school database," he said breezily, flicking to the next page of his comic.

"And?"

"I changed all the grades on my report card to straight As."

"You *what?*" I gasped.

It didn't surprise me that Alexis could break through any password walls the school had set up to protect their database. He was the best at technology in the school and Mrs. Prime was always whining to Dad about Alexis's "wasted potential" due to his inclination to use his computer whizz-kid skills to break the rules and cause chaos, rather than use his savvy talent for "the greater good," as she put it.

But as far as Alexis was concerned, causing chaos at school *was* for the greater good.

"Got away with it for a couple of weeks at least. Sadly, that new Mr. Mercury is a bit more with it than I thought. Turns out he was reviewing a few things and spotted the error. He'd originally given me a D so he flagged it up to the rest of the staff. I underestimated him. I probably could have made the change in grades a bit subtler, but whatever." Alexis sighed. "I'm grounded for two weeks."

"Cool." Clara nodded in awe.

"Aurora!" Dad's voice came floating up the stairs. "You need to let Kimmy out; she's bursting to go."

Alexis slid his headphones back on and returned his attention to his comic book, while Clara happily skipped along the corridor to her room and I made my way downstairs, swinging myself around the end of the banister and into the kitchen, where I was almost knocked to the floor by my very enthusiastic German shepherd.

"Hey, Kimmy!" I laughed, kneeling to greet her properly and gasping for air in between her slobbery licks. "Did you miss me today?"

"She rolled in my dahlias," Dad informed me, pulling out a stack of plates from the cupboard and setting them down on the side. "They were flowering beautifully."

"Kimmy," I said to her in my firmest voice as she sat down obediently in front of me, her tongue lolling out, "is that true? Did you roll in Dad's dahlias?"

She tilted her head.

"I see. It was an accident?"

She tilted her head the other way.

"You'll try your best never to do it again?"

She plonked her right paw on my leg.

"And you're very sorry?"

She leaned forward and gave me a big lick. I looked up at Dad as a smile broke across his face and he reached down to pat Kimmy's head. She nuzzled his leg in response.

Dad is always trying to be strict with Kimmy but, in the end, he's as much a sucker for her big, shiny brown eyes and goofy expression as I am.

"You're a real pair," he chuckled, shaking his head and pulling on the oven mitts. "All right, Kimmy, I forgive you."

"Where's Mum?" I asked, straightening up and brushing the dog hairs off my uniform while Kimmy ran off to get her ball.

"She's stuck at work," Dad said in a strained voice. "She'll be back soon. Hopefully in time for dinner. Go on, take Kimmy into the garden. And keep her away from my plants!"

While Kimmy happily peed on what was left of Dad's dahlias, I stood in the middle of the garden thinking about Mum. Recently my parents had been quite snappy with each other and things had felt a bit tense between them. Mum usually had this way of making Dad laugh until he cried, but that hadn't happened for ages.

I had mentioned this to Alexis, but he told me not to worry about it and said that it was just because Mum was working really long hours at the moment and had to do a lot of business traveling. According to Alexis, the reason they were getting angry about it was because Dad missed having her around and Mum missed being around, so it was actually a *good* thing that they were mad, as it showed they cared.

Which I guess made sense.

After a few rounds of fetch with her old mangled tennis ball, I brought Kimmy inside and helped Dad set the table. Dad called Alexis and Clara to come downstairs and as we waited for Mum, he decided to keep us occupied by telling us about this big exhibition coming up at the Natural History Museum where he works. He's a professor of mineralogy, which means he knows everything about dirt and rocks and stuff.

"Here, I picked up twelve copies," he said, showing us page seven of the newspaper as we took our places round the table.

A GEM OF AN EXHIBITION OPENING AT THE NATURAL HISTORY MUSEUM, read the headline, with a photo beside it of Dad beaming. He was holding a box containing what looked like a bunch of stones.

"These precious stones are centuries old!" Dad informed us eagerly. "They've been discovered by explorers, buried and lost in the earth. I've been studying the markings for

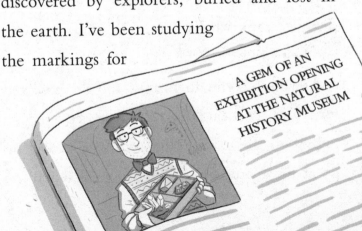

A GEM OF AN EXHIBITION OPENING AT THE NATURAL HISTORY MUSEUM

weeks, but I won't give it all away! You'll have to wait for the big opening night to read all about them. Everyone's invited – it's a special black-tie event. Alexis, we can get you your first tuxedo!"

Alexis rolled his eyes, but Clara was much more interested. She was the smartest student in her year, and had already skipped a grade. Although she's only seven, she's always reading; her brain can store a load of facts about all different types of things. Mum likes to say she's a mini version of Dad. She even got his strong eyebrows, curious, wide eyes, and a forehead constantly furrowed in concentration.

"We get to go to the opening night?" Clara asked, pulling the article toward her.

"Of course! I'm in charge of the exhibition, so my whole family has to be there," he said, puffing out his chest proudly.

"Can Kimmy come?" I asked, as she pawed at my leg. "I can make sure she has a bath for the occasion."

"As much as I'd love her there, I'm afraid no dogs are allowed in the museum; too many bones on display," Dad said with a chuckle. "Sorry, Kimmy."

I consoled her with a pat on her head and a whispered promise that I'd give her some of my dinner to make up for it. The timer on the oven went off and, just as Dad slid the vegetable quiche onto the table, Mum came bursting through the door.

"Hi, everyone!" she beamed.

Alexis's fork fell from his hand with a loud clatter, Clara stared with her mouth wide open and Dad dropped an oven mitt.

"Mum," I began, cutting through the shocked silence, "what *happened* to you?"

Her normally glossy long brown hair was

sticking up in all directions, like some big fuzz ball on top of her head, and small plumes of smoke rose from the ends. There was what looked like a scorch mark down her cheek and a sweep of charcoal across her forehead. She looked like she'd been struck by lightning.

At first, she was confused by our reaction to her entrance, but then she picked up a large silver serving spoon from the table to examine her reflection.

"I don't know what you're all— OH MY GOODNESS ME!" Her free hand shot to her frazzled hair and she began

#BEST MUM EVER

to desperately attempt to pat it down. "It's all that ... hot yoga!"

"Hot yoga?" I repeated. Mum had never been into yoga or anything like that before.

But then, she was really good at all sports, so maybe hot yoga was her new fitness thing. Sadly, she had not passed those sporty genes to me. Although, I could totally relate to her current uncontrollable, frizzy hair. That was my permanent look.

"Yes, I've been trying hot yoga out." Mum laughed nervously. "Great for a workout but perhaps not too good for my hair. Next time, I'll have to wear a shower cap or something."

"Who knew hot yoga could be so lethal?" Alexis said under his breath as Mum tried to rub off the scorch marks with a dish towel.

The fumes billowing up from Mum's hair reached the smoke detector above the kitchen door and it responded with a loud wail. Dad leapt up to help Mum as she began flapping the dish towel at the alarm, which gave Kimmy the perfect opportunity to jump up to the table and grab the quiche between her jaws. She smoothly whipped the whole thing off its plate and raced full pelt into the garden with it to do a victory lap, causing bits of pastry and egg to go flying across the grass.

"KIMMY, *nooooooooo!*" Dad yelped, running after her and leaving Mum trying to hit the disable button on the smoke alarm.

I honestly didn't think my family could get any more bonkers.

I was very, very wrong.

A week later, the light-beam thing happened again.

Our nosy neighbor, Mrs. Crow, immediately popped her head up from the other side of the garden fence to see what was going on.

"Oh my! Gerald! GERALD!" she shrieked to her husband, who swung open an upstairs window and craned his neck over the windowsill.

"What is it?" he asked grumpily. "I'm in the middle of clarinet practice."

"It's an alien invasion! I saw it! I saw it!" she cried. "A blinding flash of light in next door's garden! It was so powerful, it nearly knocked down our fence! It blew me right over onto my bottom!"

"Why are you talking about bottoms?" he asked, twiddling with his hearing aid.

"I'm calling the *Weekly Herald*!" Mrs. Crow yelled, running across her patio toward the door. "Can you believe it? An alien invasion, right next door! This is front page stuff!"

I was frozen to the spot where I had fallen backward, until I heard Dad cough. I looked up to see that he was standing with Mum right behind me. His eyes were wide with shock. Weirdly, Mum's were filled with excitement.

"Aurora," Dad whispered, as Kimmy barked at the empty garden. "Could you come inside for a moment? I think we need to talk."

Uh-oh. I was in BIG trouble.

I obviously didn't plan on this happening when I got home from school. I was actually planning on perfecting my cartwheel. Everyone in my class can do them except me. Suzie does the best cartwheels in the whole school. She makes it look like it is no effort at all, stepping forward precisely before neatly ducking her head and swinging her legs swiftly round through the air above her and finishing with her arms pointed up like a professional gymnast.

"Well done, Suzie!" Miss Nimble, our PE teacher, had exclaimed earlier that day, as she

watched Suzie cartwheel across her gym mat with ease. "You are as elegant as a gazelle leaping across the plain!"

Her gaze then drifted toward me at the other end of the gym as I took an enthusiastic run-up, dived forward and belly flopped onto my mat with a loud **THUD**.

Suzie and her friends burst into hysterical laughter and Kizzy ran over to help, prodding my cheek and asking if I was dead or alive.

So when I got home I was determined to practice a cartwheel until I could do it and then I would show everyone at school the next day. It was one of the

rare occasions that Mum and Dad were both home early, but they were talking in their serious voices in the sitting room. Alexis shut himself in his room as usual and Clara was at a friend's house for the afternoon, so I had the garden to myself.

I gave Kimmy a cuddle and left her chewing a new toy in the kitchen before marching through to the garden determinedly. I lifted my hands in the air before falling forward with gusto, but my feet barely left the ground. It was more of a sideways roll. I tried again, but the second attempt was even worse and the third, worse than that. After the fourth time, I was ready to give up altogether.

I sighed. Why was I the ONLY person in the world who couldn't do a cartwheel? It was so *unfair*! If Suzie had been there, she would have been shrieking with laughter.

I felt the frustration bubbling up angrily

inside me and my cheeks grew hot as I remembered Suzie laughing and pointing at me after my humiliating belly flop. Why did she always have to be so *mean*? I bet she'd told the whole gymnastics team by now. And they'd have told her about my weird scar obsession. They must think I'm the biggest freak EVER.

My eyes pricked with hot tears and that was when I felt this surge of energy come rushing through my body, shooting down my arms, making my fingers feel fiery and tingling, and suddenly...

WHOOSH!

Sparks flew from my fingertips and rays of bright light came bursting out from my palms, nearly stripping the garden of its grass, and knocking over the birdbath. As the beams suddenly cut out, I stumbled backward, tripping over my feet and falling onto the ground. Kimmy came running through from the kitchen to stand over me protectively and bark madly with her ears up, unsure as to what was going on.

As Mrs. Crow shrieked wildly, I considered blaming this on a freak lightning strike or perhaps going along with her alien theory.

That was obviously before I knew Mum and Dad had witnessed the entire thing.

I stood up and followed them nervously through to the sitting room, plonking myself down on the sofa opposite. Kimmy refused to leave my side, sensing that something was up. She placed herself next to my feet, still completely alert, and I began stroking

her soft ears for comfort.

"Mum, Dad, you may have noticed that I almost accidentally blew up the garden but—"

"Oh, honey," Mum beamed, leaning forward. "I'm so *proud* of you."

I blinked back at her. *Huh?*

"Aurora," Dad said carefully, "has anything else happened recently? Anything a bit … strange?"

I nodded.

"When I saw Clara being picked on the other day," I admitted quietly. "I stopped them by … well, seeing Clara look

so upset, I just felt something bubbling up in my stomach and then I got all hot and it was like fire was running through my veins and then light sparked from my fingertips. That was how I felt just now too. I didn't mean to ruin the garden, I promise."

"Clara was being picked on?" Dad asked in concern. "Why didn't you tell us?"

"Aurora," Mum began in this gentle voice, "I know you must be feeling scared right now. And confused."

"Well, yeah. I asked Mrs. Damsel about the signs of growing pains, but she didn't say anything about sparks or light beams."

"It isn't growing pains," Mum interrupted softly. She turned to Dad. "We *need* to tell her."

He let out a long sigh and then nodded, looking deflated.

"Tell me what?" I asked curiously.

"Aurora," she began. "We have ... *superpowers*."

Silence roared through the room as she waited for my reaction. After a few moments, I started laughing.

"Nice one, Mum," I giggled, impressed at how good she was at keeping a straight face.

She exchanged a worried glance with Dad.

"Aurora, I'm not joking."

I looked from Mum's serious expression to Dad. He was nodding slowly. I stopped laughing, my breath catching in my throat.

"W... what?"

"All the women in our family can control light and energy. Your powers are beginning to come through. Very early, I must admit; my powers didn't start showing themselves until much later, after I'd left school—"

"Wait a second..." I held up my hands. Dad ducked, throwing himself flat against the sofa and covering his head with his arms.

"Oh really," Mum scolded, as he peeked at me through his fingers. "She's perfectly in control of her powers right now."

"Sorry. Past experience," he said pointedly at Mum, sitting up and readjusting his sweater.

"I have ... superpowers?" I whispered, lowering my gaze to my hands. The tingling in my fingers was slowly beginning to ebb away, but now my whole body started to feel numb as I tried to take in what Mum was saying.

"Yes," Mum said and smiled. "It's time to tell you how it all came about. It's a long story."

"I don't think Aurora needs to hear the story right now. She's got enough to deal with," Dad huffed.

"Of course she needs to know," Mum told him through gritted teeth, before taking a deep breath and facing me. "A long, long time ago, a great darkness descended over the world. We still don't know why, but can you imagine a world with no light? Pitch-black, desolate, cold. The only light left was the aurora borealis, otherwise known as the northern lights, and even they were fading."

"Kiyana," Dad sighed, running a hand through his hair, "please can we—"

"While everyone else lost hope," Mum continued, talking over him, "a brave young girl named Dawn decided to try and do something about it. She was tired of watching her people suffer. She believed that the last remaining light in the world might be the key to saving it, but no one listened to her. Dawn wasn't going to let that stop her. She began to make her way to the aurora borealis. The journey was very tough, and many times, Dawn wanted to give up, but her courage kept her going. When Dawn got to the northern lights, tired and cold, with no energy left, the lights were glowing brighter than they had ever shone. That's when she found it, the—"

"That's enough, Kiyana!" Dad snapped, standing up and coming over to sit next to me, placing a hand on mine and squeezing it. "This is all too much. Aurora, do you want me to get you a glass of water?"

"She's stronger than you think she is," Mum protested. "She needs to hear—"

"Hear what? A bunch of legends and myths that have been twisted and changed over the years like a game of telephone?" Dad took a deep breath as Mum pursed her lips. "Kiyana, even you don't know what is the truth and what is fiction. Let's just keep things simple for now."

"What does this Dawn person have to do with anything?" I asked, my heart slamming against my chest. This had to be some kind of weird joke. Except Mum and Dad weren't laughing.

"You're a descendent of Dawn," Mum said eagerly before Dad could stop her. "All the women in our family have superpowers. Passed on since Dawn Beam restored light to the world. Her powers have passed down to every generation, to me and now to you." She paused and then added quickly, "Her powers *and* her surname. For which you can be grateful, since your father's surname was Bogglebog."

Dad mumbled under his breath about the great legacy of the Bogglebogs and their role in the invention and development of the flyswatter. We both ignored him.

"I don't understand," I said slowly, my head starting to hurt with all this crazy information. "You're telling me that I have superpowers … and so do you?"

Mum nodded. "All those times I've been away on business trips; I was, in fact, saving the world."

"*All* those times?"

"Every single one of them. Oh, and ... uh ... well, that hot yoga class the other day." She smiled at me guiltily. "A criminal tried to destroy some evidence that would put him in prison, but I managed to rescue it at the expense of my hair. He had fashioned a hair dryer into a destructive weapon, which, come to think of it, was actually quite imaginative for a bad guy, but the downfall was that he needed electricity. So, after dodging a few of his badly aimed shots at me, I just *pulled the plug* on that one."

She burst out laughing at her joke. Dad coughed. I stared at her.

"Get it? I saved the day, but otherwise it might have been a bit of a *hair*-y situation."

Again, silence roared through the room.

"Wow. Tough crowd. Anyway," she shrugged, "now that your powers are showing, it's time for you to begin your training so that you can become a superhero too, and save the world alongside me."

Wait. *What*? Me?! A *superhero??* SAVING THE WORLD?? Superpowers are one thing, but a *superhero*?

I can't even do a cartwheel.

HOW CAN I SAVE THE WORLD WHEN I CAN'T EVEN DO A CARTWHEEL?

Dad cleared his throat as I sat there freaking out, a hundred questions clouding my brain. I mean, besides not being able to do a cartwheel, I kicked a ball at a teacher's head. How can I be a superhero when I kick balls at teachers' heads?? That's surely not a very superhero thing to do. And do I have to wear a cape now?! Superheroes wear capes, right? Would I get to pick the color of the cape? Suzie would think I was a WAY bigger freak if I walked around school wearing a cape! Do superheroes even still go to school?! Do superheroes have school friends?? Do I have to make up a silly superhero name, like Lightblaster Girl?!?! I don't want to be Lightblaster Girl!! THIS IS A TOTAL DISASTER!

I sat in shock, barely blinking.

"It's a lot to take in," Mum admitted, her big brown eyes filled with concern as she watched me. "Are you OK, Aurora?"

Hmm. Let me think on that one. Am I OK? *Am. I. OK.*

AM I OK??? ARE YOU KIDDING ME??

Let's just take a moment to recap on everything that's just occurred in the last few minutes of my life, shall we?

1. Light beams keep **exploding** from my hands
2. I found out my mum is a **superhero**
3. I found out that I am descended from a long line of **female superheroes**

4. Which means Grandma was probably one too

5. Which means she's probably not retired in Cornwall, living a peaceful life running a rescue shelter for stray chickens like she said

6. I found out I have **superpowers**

7. I have to train up these aforementioned **superpowers**

8. I might have to wear a cape

9. Despite the whole superhero thing, I still can't do a cartwheel

10. **MY WHOLE LIFE HAS BEEN A LIE**

The doorbell buzzed suddenly, making us all jump. Dad got up tentatively and went to see who it was, while Mum came over to sit next to me, gripping my hand and refusing to take her eyes off me.

"Nothing's really changed, Aurora," she

whispered. "You're still you and I'm still me."

"Hello, sir!" We heard a man's enthusiastic voice ring down the hallway as Dad opened the door. "I'm from the *Weekly Herald*! There's allegedly been a hostile alien strike in your back garden. Do you have any comments to make about our impending doom?"

"You know what, Mum? I think you may be wrong," I whispered, as we heard Dad shutting the door in the reporter's face.

I brought my eyes up to meet hers.

"I have a feeling that *everything* has changed."

I tried to get out of going to school the next day, but Dad was adamant that I had to carry on as normal.

"It's important that you keep a healthy life balance," he said sternly, like he was Oprah or something. He pulled the duvet off me and got my uniform out.

I hadn't really managed any sleep. After the reporter left the night before, Dad had made me a cup of tea and banned Mum from "overwhelming" me with any more "stories."

Alexis had then come slumping down the stairs in search of snacks, with his noise-canceling headphones still on. Luckily, he hadn't noticed or heard a thing over his blaring music. He took in Mum holding my hand, Kimmy sitting alertly at my feet, and Dad placing a mug of tea in front of me. He slid his headphones down from his ears, folding his arms as he leaned on the door frame with a bemused expression on his face.

"Did Aurora fall into the toilet again or something?"

If I hadn't been stumped into silence by Mum's big superhero reveal, I would have told him that had happened ONE TIME and it was in the middle of the night so it was all dark and it was just because *someone* had left the toilet seat up. And it was deeply traumatic so I didn't appreciate him making light of that particular incident, especially as it was HIS FAULT that it happened to me in the first place.

But I was totally freaking out and in too much shock to speak, so he got off lightly with that comment.

The doorbell went again and Dad grumbled about nosy reporters, but it turned out to be Clara being dropped off by her friend's mum.

"Welcome home, squirt," we heard Alexis say after he went to let her in. "Everyone's in the sitting room being weird."

"What's new?" Clara sighed, wandering through to us and crossing her arms. "Dad, can I go to science camp this summer? Ruby is going and she says that—"

"Let's discuss that another time, shall we?" Dad said chirpily, covering the situation by clapping his hands together and making Kimmy leap to her feet in excitement. "Who's hungry? How about I make pancakes?"

Clara and Alexis shared a confused look. Dad only ever made pancakes on special occasions and usually for breakfast, rather than for dinner.

"OK." Alexis shrugged, deciding not to probe further. "Pancakes sound good."

"And while I make the pancakes, I can tell you more interesting facts about my precious stone exhibition! You can hear all the behind-the-scenes gossip."

"Any chance we can get the pancakes without the museum chat?" Alexis mumbled, but Dad was already in the kitchen, clattering the frying pans and ordering Clara to hunt down the flour.

Alexis followed them out, while I sat numbly on the sofa and Mum continued to squeeze my hand and whisper how exciting everything was, how I wasn't to worry, it would all be OK.

I hardly heard her. My ears were ringing and my mouth had gone all dry, making it difficult to swallow. The whole room felt hazy and my brain didn't seem to be functioning properly.

MUM was a superhero? I had *superpowers*? ME? This was all wrong. There was nothing special about me. I wasn't the superhero type. I'm just normal and boring. I *can't* have superpowers. It didn't make any sense.

Yet, sparks had flown out of my fingers. Twice. I had seen it. I had felt it. What else could explain that?

And when I really thought about it, it did kind of make sense that Mum hadn't actually been traveling for work all those times. She had always left for her "business trips" at the last minute, without any warning, and she had never gone with a suitcase or a laptop or anything. The hot yoga thing too – NOBODY got actual scorch marks and sizzling hair from hot yoga. I can't believe we fell for that one.

But *saving the world*? *My mum, a superhero*? My mum who never knew what day it was; who often put important letters and bills in the fridge for safekeeping; who sang the *Britain's Got Talent* theme tune way too loudly and out of tune in the shower every morning. My mum, who once cheered me up after a bad day by putting a pair of trousers on her head and shoes on her hands.

THAT'S WHO WE ARE ENTRUSTING TO SAVE THE WORLD???

If so, we're all in trouble.

But then again, she *did* win the parents' race at sports day really easily. She wasn't even out of breath and was way ahead of the others. Also, there was that time she hit the ball so hard in a tennis game, it flew out of the court and right across a big field. So maybe she is a superhero after all.

I just thought she had an unusually strong forehand, like Serena Williams.

The rest of the evening had felt like a blur. I barely touched my food and couldn't concentrate on any of the conversation. I didn't even protest when Alexis reached over and slid a pancake off my plate onto his without asking. When I went to bed, I just lay there, staring up at the ceiling. At one point, I thought that maybe this whole thing had been a really odd dream, so I purposefully rolled off the bed to see if that woke me up. It didn't. I landed with a loud thump on the floor. This was not a dream. This was happening.

And now my arm hurt on top of everything else.

★

"Everything OK?" Kizzy asked, making me jump when she found me staring into space by my locker.

Dad had just dropped me off at the gates, having made me promise to call him immediately if anything "strange or dangerous" happened.

Which, by the way, *filled* me with confidence.

"What do you mean? I'm fine!" I replied to Kizzy, a little too enthusiastically. "I'm absolutely fine! Everything's fine! I'm normal! Just a normal eleven-year-old! Just a normal everyday person! Normal! Person! That's what I am!"

"Whoa, OK!" Kizzy laughed, linking her arm through mine. "You just looked in a bit of a daze, that's all. Are you looking forward to the assembly?"

"Huh?"

"Mr. Mercury's assembly." Her eyes widened in surprise as I stared at her blankly. "The one about your dad's new exhibition?"

"Oh. Right. The precious stones. Yes."

Every now and then we had these assemblies where a teacher would give a presentation on an interesting topic, or the choir would get up and sing songs from a West End musical or something. I'd forgotten that Mr. Mercury was doing a science one today.

"Are you sure you're OK?" Kizzy asked slowly. "You seem . . . distracted."

"I'm fine! I'm great. I don't know why you keep asking that. I'm totally groovy."

Totally groovy. *Totally groovy*?! That's what I went with?! TOTALLY GROOVY?! I have never used the word "groovy" IN MY LIFE. Who uses the word groovy?! No one in this century, that's for sure.

"Um. Good. Glad you're . . . *groovy*," she

nodded, trying and failing to hide a smile.

Kizzy was still looking at me curiously as we sat down in one of the back rows of the school hall and Mr. Mercury got up to stand at the podium. I did try and concentrate on what he was saying because it was my dad's project, but thanks to Mr. Mercury's monotone voice, it was hard to pay attention and I had all these thoughts running through my head, like...

I have superpowers. My mum is a superhero. I'm descended from superheroes. This can't be happening. I have superpowers. What is going on? How has this happened? Do I have to wear a cape? My mum is a superhero. How do I make the light beams come out of my hands? Do I have to say a special command, like "shazam" or something? Or do a weird hand pose like Spider-Man? I can't believe I fell for the hot yoga thing. People would sue if hot yoga gave them scorch marks. I am so gullible. People with superpowers surely shouldn't be as gullible as I am. You can't have a gullible superhero. Not that I am a superhero. Am I? If I have superpowers, does that automatically make me a superhero? What happens if I'm a super villain? Can you choose which one, or are you just assigned a "hero" or "villain" title, like in basketball when you're just given a position and someone to guard? I can't believe this is happening. What am I going to do? As if this is—

"Aurora Beam? Aurora?"

Kizzy jabbed me sharply in the ribs with her elbow.

"Ow! What?" I hissed.

She nodded toward Mr. Mercury at the front of the hall. The whole school had swiveled round in their seats and was looking at me expectantly.

"Uh ... yes, I'm present!"

A ripple of sniggers passed across the hall. Suzie

Bravo, a few rows in front, sighed impatiently.

"Ah, well, I wasn't actually doing a roll call," Mr. Mercury said.

"Oh." My cheeks grew hot with embarrassment. "What was the question?"

"I was just saying how your father is curating these unique gems which are going on display at the Natural History Museum in a few weeks," he explained slowly into the microphone. "I wondered if you'd like to say anything about them, as your family is so involved with such a remarkable discovery?"

"Nope," I squeaked, sinking down into my seat. "I'm good."

Mr. Mercury tutted. "All right, then. Well, as I was saying, I am very grateful to Aurora's dad, Professor Beam, for allowing me to take the Year Sevens on a special school trip to the museum later this term. If anyone has any questions..."

Now that the attention of the entire student body was no longer on me, I zoned out again. I began to examine my hands. They looked like normal hands. I squinted down at my fingers, scrutinizing them closely. Apart from the swirled scar on my left palm, they could have been anyone's hands. There was no sign that these hands were superpower hands. Nothing that showed that these hands could shoot out powerful light beams that knocked over birdhouses. No sign that—

"Hello! Earth to Aurora!!"

I jumped as Kizzy's voice cut sharply through my concentration. The assembly had finished and everyone was already filing out, while I had just been sitting there, staring at my hands. One of the girls who had picked on Clara the other day happened to be in the row in front of us and began sniggering as I hurriedly dropped my hands and stood up.

"Admiring your weird scar again, are you? It's about as interesting as the rock display your dad is putting on," she sneered, nudging the boy next to her. They burst out laughing before sauntering out of the hall.

"Ignore them," Kizzy said. "They're just jealous because your dad has such a cool job."

We both knew she was lying, but I smiled at her gratefully anyway.

I got told off for not paying attention by four different teachers throughout the day, and in PE I got hit in the face by a basketball because at the time I was staring down at my feet wondering if I could shoot light beams out of my toes too.

When school *finally* finished, I shoved my books back in my locker, slamming it shut quickly before they all fell out again.

"Hey, honey!"

I screamed as I closed my locker door and Mum was standing there right behind it, beaming at me.

"WHAT THE... MUM! You gave me a heart attack! How did you get there without me seeing you?!"

She held up her hands and wiggled her fingers gleefully. "Duh! Superhero!"

"That isn't funny!" I hissed, checking no one could overhear. "What are you doing here?"

"You're coming with me today. Your dad is picking up Alexis and Clara."

"What? Why?

Where are we going?"

"It's time."

"Time for what?"

A mischievous grin broke across Mum's face.

"Time, Aurora Beam, to see what you can do."

In movies, superheroes always have glamorous underground lairs where they keep all their awesome state-of-the-art training equipment, flashy cars and weapons.

In reality, it turns out that superheroes learn how to use their powers in empty parking lots.

"What is that smell?" I asked, wrinkling my nose as Mum picked up an empty soda can and threw it toward the trash can at the other end of the parking lot. It went straight in.

"Stop being so fussy, Aurora – this is a perfect spot to begin your training. Plenty of space and it's nice and quiet so you can really focus." She watched me carefully as I folded my arms. "How are you feeling?"

"OK." I shrugged.

"Hard to concentrate at school, right?"

"A little."

"When your grandmother first told me I had superpowers, I was so confused and terrified I shut myself in my closet and refused to come out for an entire day. Mum had to lure me out with the smell of fresh chocolate brownies that she wafted in from outside the door. Trust me, I know what you're going through. Although, I was a little older than you are. Your powers have shown themselves very early compared to others in our family." She paused thoughtfully. "I wonder why."

"So, I'm *doubly* weird!" I whined. "Weird

because of the powers and even weirder because I'm not meant to have them yet."

"Weird is not the word I'd use. I'd say you were very, very special."

"You have to say that – you're my mum," I huffed, rolling my eyes. "What are we doing here?"

"This is superhero training, lesson number one. We're going to work on controlling your powers, so they don't just explode whenever they want to. Then we need to find out what other powers you have."

"Wait, I have other powers? I thought you said the women in our family can all control light."

"That's right, but we seem to have extra individual ... perks, if you will." She smiled. "They're not extra superpowers, we just sort of excel in other areas too. In addition to controlling light, I'm pretty strong and fast.

Very helpful with superhero duties. Your grandmother has some kind of healing capability. She can't exactly heal wounds, but she can make pain fade when she's near."

"And Aunt Lucinda?"

Mum grimaced at the mention of her sister. They had never really gotten along.

"Charm. She's superior at persuading anyone to do exactly what she wants," Mum said disapprovingly. "Useful when it comes to breaking the law."

"What do you think my extra perk is?"

She looked at me thoughtfully. "I don't know, but there's something about you. . . We'll work out what it is. It might develop at a later stage in life. I only started winning races when I was in college. Once we've worked on you controlling your superpowers, we can start focusing on what else you can do to help save the world. Hopefully, it will be something that comes in very handy when going up against criminals!"

"Mum, can I ask you something?"

"Anything."

"How do you know when to go save the world?"

She gave me a funny look. "What do you mean?"

"All those times you went off on your 'business trips,' how did you know that there was something bad going on that you needed to stop? Do we have an inbuilt superhero radar or something?"

Mum burst out laughing. "No, Aurora, we don't."

"Well, then, how do you know there's a bad guy about to attack?"

She took a deep breath. "I have help when it comes to that side of things. I'm kept in the know when there's something fishy going on out there."

"Like some kind of secret network?"

"Let's just focus on training your superpowers for now, OK? One day I'll tell you how everything works, but for now, I just want to make sure you can keep your powers under control."

She reached out her hand to give mine a comforting squeeze before dropping it and marching determinedly to the middle of the empty parking lot, turning back to face me.

"Right," she said, rubbing her hands together excitedly. "Let's get started."

I nodded, attempting to ignore the butterflies fluttering about uncontrollably in my stomach.

"Come forward a little," Mum instructed. "That's it, so I don't have to shout. Now, take a deep breath. In through your nose, out through your mouth. In through your nose, out through your mouth. In through your—"

I interrupted her with a fit of spluttering.

"Sorry!" I wheezed, as she rushed over to clap me on the back. "I think I inhaled a bug."

"Up your nose?!"

"In my mouth."

"You were supposed to be inhaling through your nose."

"I thought I was inhaling through my mouth and out through my nose."

"Weren't you listening?" Mum laughed. "*In* through your *nose, out* through your *mouth*."

"You see? I can't even breathe right!" I wailed. "Mum, are you sure I have superpowers? I've been thinking about this all day and I am SO not superhero material. Surely someone like Suzie Bravo or Georgie Taylor would be better for the job. They're cool and popular and perfect. Maybe the beams of light are something else; maybe they really are just growing pains and I'm a big freak." I let out a long sigh. "I think there has been a mistake."

"You think being cool, popular and perfect are the qualities you need to be a superhero? You really do have a lot to learn." Mum raised an eyebrow at me. "Trust me, there has not been a mistake. Now, stop this negativity, please, otherwise it will never work. Shoulders back, relax and take a nice deep breath. In through your..."

She gestured for me to finish her sentence.

"Nose," I smiled weakly.

"Very good!" She laughed, moving back to her starting position. "The breathing is to relax you. You need to focus on how you felt when your powers came to you before. How you felt in the garden and how you felt on the playground the other day. You need to channel that energy, so that your powers get going. Once you know how to form them, we can train you to control them."

I looked down at my hands and wiggled

my fingers.

"I have no idea," I admitted. "It all just . . . happened."

"Try," Mum encouraged. "Take your time and try."

I wiggled my fingers more enthusiastically. I closed my eyes, scrunched up my face and focused all my energy on getting light beams to spark from my fingertips. I bent my knees and held my hands out in front of me, shaking my arms around madly and still wiggling my fingers, keeping my eyes tightly shut in concentration.

"SHHHHHHAAAAAAAAABEEEEEEEAAAAAAAMMMMMMM!" I yelled.

Nothing happened.

I opened one eye to see Mum with her hand clapped over her mouth and her eyes watering as she tried not to laugh.

"Did you just say ... **SHABEAM?**"

She exploded into hysterical giggles, bending over double and clutching her stomach. I dropped my hands and stood up straight, my face flushing with heat as I waited for her to stop laughing.

"Sorry, I'm sorry." She grinned, wiping the tears from her eyes, her shoulders still shaking. "You should have seen you! Crouching in that position and making those faces! And then you ... then you said ... **SHABEAM!**"

She burst into a fresh round of giggles. I narrowed my eyes at her.

"Well, I don't know!" I huffed. "My powers aren't working!"

"**SHABEAM** isn't a word," she chuckled, now

fanning her face with her hand as she tried to pull herself together. "**SHABEAM!**"

"It's not that funny, Mum!" I protested, the irritation rising up inside me.

"I'm not laughing at you, darling, I promise. You did really well," she said, grinning. "You just looked like you were warming up for some kind of bizarre wrestling match or something. I wasn't expecting you to do ... well ... that!"

"You *are* laughing at me. I was trying to get my powers working," I argued. "And **SHABEAM** is a totally normal word!"

I shouldn't have said "**SHABEAM**" again, it just set Mum off on another round of giggles. Honestly, she's supposed to be the grown-up in this situation. And OK, so maybe saying "**SHABEAM**" was a bit weird, but no weirder than Harry Potter saying spells and stuff, right? How am I meant to know what to say? **SHABEAM** just felt right in the moment.

Like *shazam* but with a personal edge.

OK, so the more I thought about it, the more embarrassed I felt about the whole **SHABEAM** thing.

WHY did I have to say **SHABEAM**? I could have said something a bit cooler. Suzie would NEVER say something like **SHABEAM**. If she suddenly got superpowers, she would probably just click her fingers and make the powers appear again with no problem whatsoever. She wouldn't stand in the middle of an empty parking lot with her bonkers mother, squatting like a chicken and yelling "**SHABEAM**."

Brilliant. Now, the word **SHABEAM** is going to haunt me for life.

My face grew hotter as my frustration at myself grew and I felt my whole body tense, and then a familiar tingling feeling race down my arms and suddenly...

WHOOSH!

The parking lot lit up in a blinding bright light as beams radiated from my hands and, almost as quickly as they had shot out, disappeared again. I snapped my head up to see Mum jumping up and down on the spot, clapping her hands together.

"That's it! You did it!" she cried, rushing over to give me a hug.

"I did?" I held out my hands as she released them and saw they were shaking. "I felt annoyed at myself for the **SHABEAM** thing."

Mum pursed her lips in an attempt not to laugh again at my use of the word "**SHABEAM**," and nodded enthusiastically.

"That's your trigger. You felt annoyed at those kids bullying Clara. And in the garden..."

"I was frustrated that I couldn't do a cartwheel," I explained. "So you think it only happens when I'm angry at something?"

"No, I think it's triggered by strong emotions,

like the buildup of pressure in the atmosphere just before a big lightning storm strikes. It just so happens you were annoyed at the bullies and then yourself. But I think when you're very happy or very sad, that will cause it too. Aurora, I need you to concentrate really hard now. It's important not to lose this moment." She held my shoulders and stood square on, looking deeply into my eyes. "I need you to remember exactly how you just felt. Focus on that overpowering feeling. Can you do that?"

"I can try."

"Good. I'm going to stand over here. Deep breath," she advised, stepping backward.

"Focus, Aurora."

I closed my eyes, but instead of scrunching up my face and wiggling my arms around, I focused my mind on the warmth in my arms, the tingling sensation in my hands, the overwhelming powerful feeling rising from my toes, washing through my body. I concentrated so hard that my ears began to ring, the rest of the world becoming a muffled blur in the background.

WHOOSH!

I stumbled backward at the force of light coming out from my hands.

Mum whooped and punched the air as the beams died away, and I clenched my hands as they continued to prickle with energy. Mum came running over once again.

"Aurora," she said, beaming at me. "You did it. *You really did it!* I knew you could. How did it feel?"

"It felt ... it felt..." I searched for the word in a daze, eventually tearing my eyes from my hands to look up at her. "It felt magical."

I came home to find an ostrich in my bedroom, wearing my bathrobe as a cape.

I guess for most people, coming home to find a cape-wearing ostrich in your room might be out of the ordinary, but I knew exactly what was going on.

"Alfred?"

The ostrich, who had been admiring himself in my mirror, spun around and blinked before strutting straight past me and down the stairs, with my bathrobe floating behind him as he went. I shook my head and followed him into the sitting room where Dad was leaning on the mantelpiece looking very tired, and a lady wearing a tiara was sitting on the sofa, shaking her head at Mum.

"Really, Kiyana, when was the last time you went clothes shopping? I remember you wearing those trousers in your last year of school. It's bad enough that your husband still thinks short-sleeved shirts are the height of fashion; someone has to talk to him before it's too late and he progresses into sandals and socks."

"I'm standing right here," Dad mumbled.

Alfred the ostrich marched over to the sofa and, with a flourishing wiggle of his bottom feathers, he perched next to the lady, allowing her to tickle his neck. Then she caught sight of me hovering by the door.

"Aurora! There you are!"

"Hey, Aunt Lucinda." I smiled as she jumped up and drew me into a perfume-heavy hug, complete with air kisses.

"I hear you've been going through some … changes," she whispered, tapping the side of her nose and winking dramatically.

Aunt Lucinda is Mum's twin sister, younger by three minutes. Mum says they started arguing in the womb and have never stopped, so Aunt Lucinda's visits were pretty rare and we could never visit her because none of us ever knew where on the planet she was living, she moved around so much. She loved bright colors, clashing fashion, big sparkling jewelry and causing as much trouble as possible. And she never went anywhere without Alfred, her snobby pet ostrich and fellow mischief maker.

Mum said her wicked sister was an "amoral liability"; Dad said she was "flighty, tricky, but kind at heart"; Alexis said she was "seriously strange"; and Clara once described her as an "excessive-attention-seeking and drama-addicted flamboyant eccentric, as though plucked from the pages of Evelyn Waugh's triumphant novel *Brideshead Revisited* and placed in modern society."

I liked her.

"So," she said, sweeping an arm around me and drawing me to sit between her and Alfred on the sofa, "tell me all about these powers of yours."

Dad cleared his throat. "Lucinda, Aurora is dealing with a lot and I think that—"

"Are you able to control them yet?" she asked excitedly, ignoring Dad completely.

"Um … I'm just getting my head round everything at the moment," I began, trying to push Alfred's feathers out of my face. "Where are Alexis and Clara?"

"Out walking Kimmy," Dad answered, glancing out of the window. "Kimmy didn't take too well to Alfred prancing around her house."

Alfred jerked his head in Dad's direction and narrowed his eyes to slits.

"Now, now, Alfred, watch that temper of yours," Lucinda said sternly. "Of course you don't prance, he didn't mean it. Did you, Henry? Apologies if Alfred is a little touchy, we just got back from a jaunt in Bali and returning to the cold weather always affects his mood. Now, Aurora, your powers have shown themselves much too early. Why do you think that is, Kiyana?"

"Are you a superhero too?" I asked her, wondering if that was why she was always flitting round the world.

Lucinda threw her head back and cackled.

"A superhero? *Moi*?"

She placed a hand on her heart and shook her head, still chuckling.

"Do you think I have the time to be a superhero? No, no, I don't bother with any of that nonsense."

"But ... you have superpowers?"

In response, she wiggled her fingers and red light beams sparked from her palms.

"Wow!" I exclaimed.

"That's enough, Lucinda," Mum said with a sigh. "Alexis and Clara will be back soon."

Lucinda rolled her eyes and dropped her

hands, returning the room to its normal light.

"Well," Mum said, clapping her hands together suddenly, "thank you, Lucinda, for dropping by, but I'm sure you have a flight to catch to the other side of the world—"

"Not at all! I'm staying in the area. It will be lovely to catch up with my favorite sister."

Mum looked horrified. "What?"

"You didn't think I'd miss Henry's big exhibition at the Natural History Museum?"

Mum turned to Dad in confusion but he appeared to be as shocked as she was.

"My exhibition?" he asked, his brow furrowed.

"I saw it in the papers! Very naughty of you not to mention it, Kiyana. I've been reading all about those precious little stones and I'm terribly excited to be joining you all for the big opening night in a few weeks' time. I'm very proud of you, Henry, heading up such a wonderful discovery. I've told simply everyone that you're my dear brother-in-law – it's a lovely talking point."

"You're coming to Henry's opening night?"

"Oh, yes. I'll be in the neighborhood until then. Let's just say I have a couple of things I need to take care of. Now, it's time for Alfred and me to go, otherwise we won't make our dinner reservation." Aunt Lucinda stood up dramatically before Alfred did the same, swishing my bathrobe behind him regally and strutting to the door. "See you all tomorrow."

She stopped at the top of the stairs and turned to face me.

"Aurora, if you have any questions about your superpowers, best to come to me. Don't listen to your mum. It's not all hard work. There's plenty of fun to be had. Just you wait and see."

She grinned mischievously and swanned

from the room, slamming the door behind her.

7

Relations between Mum and Dad got worse.

When Aunt Lucinda had stayed with us in the past, the atmosphere had always been slightly tense, but this time it was different. After Aunt Lucinda and Alfred left for their dinner, Mum received a message on her phone and had grabbed her coat and rushed from the house, yelling as she ran out that we shouldn't wait up for her. Dad and I shared a look.

"Saving the world really is a full-time job,"

he said quietly, before forcing a smile and asking me if I'd like to help him cook.

Since then, she's been saving the world every weekend. Alexis, Clara and I were used to Mum dashing out for "last-minute work meetings" and returning home when we were all in bed, but now, thanks to my after-school training sessions and Lucinda dropping in whenever she felt like it – not to mention the trouble my aunt had already caused locally thanks to Alfred's habit of strolling around neighborhood driveways and pecking at random cars – Mum was even busier and Alexis began commenting on her hectic schedule.

"She's working hard, that's all," Dad told him defensively, when he mentioned that she was hardly ever in the house. "Now, what film are we going to watch? Alexis, you choose."

Dad was putting on a brave face, but I knew he was stressed about it, especially as he was so busy at the museum in the run-up to the exhibition. When Mum eventually got back in the middle of the night, they would have heated discussions in their room and I'd always hear a door slam at the end.

"It's not your fault," Kizzy told me at school, when I confessed to her that they were arguing all the time. "They'll be OK."

But what Kizzy didn't know was that it WAS my fault. If Mum wasn't so preoccupied with training me to manage my powers, then she'd have more time with Dad at home. But I couldn't tell Kizzy that.

"I knew something was up with you," Kizzy said gently, as we tied our sneakers in the locker room before PE. "You've been so out of it lately."

"Sorry." I sighed, wishing I could tell her the truth.

"Don't worry, you've got a lot on your

mind." She put her arm round me and I leaned my head on her shoulder. "Try and stay positive. We've got the castle tomorrow, so that's something good!" She pulled away and laughed at my confused expression. "Don't tell me you've forgotten about the history trip?"

"Oh, right."

"Apparently, you can try on old pieces of armor," she said brightly, standing up. "Promise me we can sit together on the bus."

"Promise."

"Pinky promise?" She held out her little finger.

UNBREAKABLE PINKY PROMISE!

I smiled and wrapped my little finger around hers, shaking it up and down.

"You can't break a pinky promise," she said knowingly as we made our way to the gym. "It's bad luck."

When school finished for the day, I expected Mum to come and get me so we could head to the parking lot. We'd been going every day after school under the guise that I was taking ballet lessons, which Alexis found HILARIOUS.

"Ballet dancers don't fall into toilets," he sniggered before Dad told him off.

I had made a little progress in my training sessions and I woke up every day looking forward to the end of school and the chance to practice my powers. After just a few days, I could now create light beams at will, even if it did take a couple of minutes. Mum thought that by next week I might be able to start learning to control the intensity of the beams. I asked her if I could change the color of my light, remembering that Lucinda's had been red, but she said that wasn't possible. Which was disappointing because it would have been super cool to be able to create a disco effect.

We still hadn't worked out what else I could do besides produce light. We tried a few tests like timing a run, jumping as high as I could and trying to lift the car, but I was useless at all of them, so it didn't look like speed or strength was my thing. I just ended up looking silly.

I did seem to be good at getting Mum to laugh at me, though, so maybe that was my extra power.

"No training session today, Aurora," Mum said when she appeared at my locker. She looked tired and her eyes were all red and squinty. "We're going straight home."

"Is everything OK?" I asked.

"Yes, of course," she replied, unconvincingly.

I followed her to the school driveway where Dad, Alexis and Clara were waiting in the car. We all sat in silence on the drive home. I looked up quizzically at Alexis, but he just shrugged back at me. When we pulled into our driveway, Dad asked us to go into the sitting room.

"OK, you guys are creeping me out. What's going on? Did Aunt Lucinda steal the crown jewels from the Tower of London again? I thought she put those back and MI5 had decided to drop the charges," Alexis said, sitting down next to me and Clara.

"This isn't to do with Aunt Lucinda," Dad said gently, glancing at Mum.

Kimmy came rushing through from the kitchen to greet me, resting her large head on my lap and letting me tickle her chin. Mum nodded at Dad encouragingly, as though giving him the go-ahead to say whatever he was trying to.

"Your mother and I have decided to separate," Dad said quietly.

I stopped playing with Kimmy's ears.

"We want you to know that we are still a family," he continued. "This is not a permanent situation, it is simply while we work things out."

Mum nodded along with him. "This is absolutely no one's fault; we still love each other very much. We just need to ... have some time to sort out the best way of moving forward."

"You're separating?" I whispered, my eyes beginning to prickle with tears. Kimmy nudged my hand with her cold, wet nose.

"Yes. Dad will be staying here with you

and I'll be staying elsewhere for now. It makes sense with my work, but I'll still be here for all of you, like accompanying you to your ballet lessons, Aurora."

"Do you have any questions about anything?" Dad asked.

I looked at Alexis, but he was staring at the ground, his jaw locked shut. Clara's eyes were filled with confusion. None of us said anything.

"I just want to stress again that this is no one's fault. Your mum and I love each other and this is just a trial, until we can find a better solution. Things haven't been running as smoothly as we'd like lately, so we..."

Dad stopped mid-sentence as his eyes met mine.

"Kiyana," he said quickly, getting Mum's attention and nodding toward me.

Her eyes widened. "Aurora, why don't we

go outside for a breather? Come on."

She stood up and grabbed my hand, pulling me hurriedly through the door and down the corridor out into the garden.

"Mum, what's wro—"

"Look at your hands."

I had been so wrapped up in what they were saying that I hadn't noticed my skin was glowing. I quickly tucked my hands into my pockets.

"Strong emotions," Mum said softly. "I thought we might have another garden-style incident in the house."

"It's OK, I can't feel the tingling. I think we're safe."

She nodded. "That's good."

We stood in silence for a moment. She moved some dirt with her foot and I just stared straight ahead.

"This is all my fault."

"Aurora, no," she said sharply, gripping my arm. "It's not."

"If I didn't have these powers, then you would be home more and Dad would be happier."

"Aurora, listen to me. This separation is nothing to do with you. Or Alexis or Clara. You have to trust me."

I bit my lip, trying not to cry. Mum put an arm round me and I sniffed into her shoulder.

"I'm scared," I whispered. And I wasn't sure if I was talking about my parents' separation or my newfound ability of superpowers.

"Me too," Mum replied gently. She pulled away to bend down to my height and look me in the eye. "But it will be OK. That much I do know."

We stood outside for a bit until the glowing wasn't so obvious and went inside to find that Alexis had retreated to his room with strict instructions not to be disturbed and Clara was reading one of her favorite science fact books with Dad. Mum said we could eat whatever we liked wherever we liked this evening, so I made some toast with her and took it to my room, but every bite I had tasted like cardboard.

I gave up, put the plate down and got into my favorite pajamas, before turning off the light and crawling under the duvet. I thought about calling Kizzy but realized it was too late for phone calls, so I lay in bed staring up at the ceiling. Every time I let my mind dwell on Mum and Dad, my skin began to throb and the room would grow bright from my

glowing, hurting my eyes. I tried my best not to think about it and distract myself by reaching for a book Kizzy had lent me. Thanks to my natural light, I didn't need a flashlight to read it under the covers.

I don't know what time I fell asleep, but I must have drifted off in the early hours of the morning because I woke up with my forehead stuck to the first page of chapter five.

I yawned, removed the book from my face and blinked into the eyes of an ostrich.

"Morning!" a shrill voice said from the corner of the room.

I screamed and started, banging my head on the wall.

"Aunt Lucinda, Alfred, what are you doing in my room?" I cried, rubbing the back of my head.

"Sorry about him." Aunt Lucinda laughed, nodding toward Alfred who had now pulled his face away from mine and was pecking at my sneakers. "He still hasn't quite gotten the hang of personal space. He brought this back for you though."

She held up the remnants of my bathrobe.

"I'm afraid he had a little trouble getting it off his neck in the end and there was a minor tear."

"It's completely ripped in two!"

"Nothing a needle and thread can't fix," she said breezily, throwing the pieces into a corner. "Now, are you ready to go?"

"What? Aunt Lucinda? What are you doing here? What's going on? I have to go to school – it's the history trip today and I—"

"I thought you deserved a day off," she said. "Don't you?"

I hesitated.

"Aurora," she said gently, sitting down at the edge of my bed, careful not to disturb the bright-blue feather headdress she was wearing today, perfectly matching her blue silk dress and silver kimono. "You've just found out you have superpowers, that your mum claims to be a superhero, and now, that your parents are going through a tough patch. You deserve to have some fun and I have some wonderful ideas. If anyone needs a day off, it's you."

Her broad smile was so infectious; I couldn't help grinning back at her.

"Now, why don't you get dressed and we can sneak out of here before your parents awake from their slumber. I thought we'd start with a spot of breakfast. How do fresh strawberries, blueberry pancakes and orange juice with the best view in the country sound?"

My phone beeped and I reached for it before Alfred began pecking at it too. It was a message from Kizzy:

> See you on the bus!
> Can't wait, I've sneaked us some snacks! Xxx

"That is –" Aunt Lucinda raised her eyebrows as I read the message "– unless you'd rather spend the day in a cold, damp castle filling in a boring fact sheet?"

Aunt Lucinda was right – I needed a break. The last week had been a bit mad, and I hadn't had any time to myself. It was only a school trip and Kizzy would understand. I just wanted to get away from everything; to forget that everything at home was rubbish. Even if it was just for one day. I quickly replied before shoving my phone into the drawer of my bedside table.

> Can't come, am sick.
> Will call later xx

"Nope, I can skip school today," I assured Aunt Lucinda, jumping out of bed, darting around Alfred, who was now pinning my hair clips to his feathers, and throwing open my closet.

"Wonderful news," Aunt Lucinda said, her eyes twinkling at me. "Time to show you just how fun superpowers can be."

"What did you do?"

Kizzy's big brown eyes searched mine quizzically as we sat on the school steps, watching Suzie and Georgie teach others from our class a new dance routine during lunch break.

You mean, what didn't *I do?* I thought in response to my best friend's question, smiling to myself as I thought about my day off with Aunt Lucinda.

It had all started with Aunt Lucinda and Alfred sneaking me out of the house and into

Aunt Lucinda's flashy red convertible sports car.

"Wow!" I gasped, crouching to slide into the front seat. "When did you get this?"

"This old thing? Yesterday," she said from the driver's seat, putting on a pair of big sunglasses and offering me a pair from the glove box before tossing a pink headscarf in my lap. "We have to have the roof down because of Alfred; you'll need to put that on to protect your hair. Although, I guess with you, it won't make much of a difference…"

She laughed as I shot her a grumpy look and then, before I'd had time to tie my headscarf on, she put her foot down and we zoomed off the driveway and whizzed down our sleepy road. Alfred had made himself comfortable in the back seat and was also sporting a floral scarf round his head and a pair of reflective aviator sunglasses.

Admittedly, he looked good.

Aunt Lucinda decided we would have breakfast at the poshest restaurant in London, so we flew toward the city, gaining many envious looks as we roared along the roads. Feeling like a glamorous movie star, I turned up the music and the three of us began bopping around in our matching headscarves and sunglasses. As we pulled up at the restaurant, I felt extremely smug until I caught a glimpse of our reflections in a shop window.

I looked like someone's great-

great-grandmother. The ostrich in the back seat looked more stylish than me. And that really is saying something.

Leaving Alfred in the car with the latest issue of *Vogue* – ostriches were not allowed where we were going – we walked into the grandest restaurant I had ever seen, with polished marble floors and vases bigger than me bursting with flowers. Even though it was early, the restaurant was already busy and there was a line of people waiting to get a breakfast table. I said to Aunt Lucinda that we could go somewhere else and that was when she gave me this knowing wink and whispered, "Watch this."

Leaning against one of the pillars nonchalantly, she opened her hands and beams of bright red light exploded from her palms, sending one of the big vases nearby toppling over into a silver-plated pastry stand. As croissants and cinnamon swirls went flying dramatically across the room, the waiters and reception staff rushed over to help, encouraging their customers not to panic while diners asked about the bizarre zap of indoor lightning they could have sworn they saw behind the pillar.

During the commotion, Aunt Lucinda wrapped her fingers around my wrist and calmly swept across the floor, guiding me to an empty table before sitting down gracefully.

"You see? Superpowers are not just for saving the world," she said, laughing at my stunned expression before gaining the attention of the nearest waiter and ordering the most expensive items on the menu.

That wasn't the only time it happened either. We got into absolutely *everywhere* with Aunt Lucinda using flashes of light to distract doormen and concierge. We even managed to sneak into the VIP backstage area at one of my favorite pop star's concerts thanks to Aunt Lucinda's little trick.

But, I couldn't tell Kizzy any of that.

"If you weren't sick, what did you do all day?"

"Nothing." I shrugged. "I just wanted a break from everything."

"I'm so sorry about your parents, Aurora," Kizzy said, putting an arm round me. "Were they mad about you skipping?"

I had been prepared for Dad to be *very* angry when I walked through the door, laden with designer shopping bags, goody bags from posh London restaurants and a VIP backstage lanyard pass for *Britain's Got Talent* round my neck. But it turned out I didn't have much to worry about. Aunt Lucinda had left a message saying I was with her for the day so he was just glad I was home safe and sound, and he wasn't even that mad about me missing school.

"You're dealing with a lot," Dad had said,

rubbing my head. "It's all right. We understand you wanted to get away. Just next time, talk to us rather than skipping school, OK? We don't want you getting in trouble."

Even though I had broken my pinky promise, Kizzy was being extra nice to try and cheer me up about my parents' separation. It made me feel even guiltier about lying to her.

"You didn't miss out on the castle, anyway. The only interesting moment was when Fred Pepe set off an emergency exit alarm and we were all evacuated. Are your mum and dad both coming to parents' evening tonight?" Kizzy asked cautiously.

I nodded.

"That's a good sign – they're making an effort." Kizzy smiled encouragingly, noticing my dubious expression. "It will be *fine*."

But she was wrong. A few hours later as parent-teacher evening started, Dad and I had already been waiting forty minutes for Mum to get there when his phone beeped in his pocket.

"Here we go," he sighed, pulling his phone out and glancing at the screen. "She's going to be late and says to start without her. Come on, then. Let's see how you're getting on."

I hadn't been expecting excellent feedback judging by my recent distractions, but Dad must have already told the staff about the separation because none of them were too hard on me. Mr. Craft, my art teacher, told him I had huge potential and Miss Nimble said that although I might not have the most *natural*

sporting ability, she
was always impressed
by my perseverance.

When we got to Mr.
Mercury's table, which I
was dreading, there was a
commotion at the back of the room and I
turned around to see Aunt Lucinda floating
toward us, wearing a green ball gown and
holding a martini glass containing some kind
of bright-orange drink with a blue umbrella.
Alfred trotted along behind her wearing a
stalker hat like he was Sherlock Holmes.

Dad groaned as she approached.

"Hellooooo!" she called happily, taking a
nearby chair and swiveling it to line up next
to ours.

"What are you doing here?"

"Don't be so grumpy, Henry, it's bad for
your wrinkles. I heard Kiyana was held up at

work so I thought I'd step in." She spotted Mr. Mercury staring at her and offered him her hand. "I'm Lucinda, Aurora's aunt. Excuse my state of dress, I didn't have time to change after a day at the opera."

"N ... nice to meet you," Mr. Mercury spluttered, shaking her hand and waiting for her to rearrange her poufy gown as she sat down.

"Now," Aunt Lucinda began, taking a sip from her cocktail. "What can you say about my niece's ability?"

I slid down in my chair, wishing the ground would swallow me up as Aunt Lucinda batted her false eyelashes at a very flustered Mr. Mercury. Suzie was whispering something to Georgie over by Miss Nimble's table and they were both pointing at Alfred, who had wandered over to the windows to peck at the curtains.

"This cannot get any worse," I whispered to Dad, covering my face with my hands. "Can we go? *Please*?"

But before Dad could answer there was another ripple of gasps and whispers as someone else came through the door. I peeked through my fingers to see Mum hurrying across the room.

"Sorry I'm late!" She smiled, coming over to our table.

Mr. Mercury stared as she shook his hand enthusiastically. He was so shocked, he looked like he'd seen a ghost. Searching for somewhere to sit, Mum did a double take at her sister.

"Lucinda? What on earth are you—"

"I was standing in for you," Aunt Lucinda informed her, taking another sip of her drink and looking very bemused. "I called round and Alexis told me where you all were. I felt it my duty to see how Aurora has been getting on at school."

"Well, there was no need. Henry and I have this under control."

Dad grimaced as Mum pulled up a spare chair, the sound of the legs screeching across the floor, reverberating through the silence of the room.

"What's wrong?" Mum asked in confusion, glancing worriedly around at all the other parents and students staring at her.

"Mum?" I squeaked, unable to bear another moment. "Your ... hair."

"What?" she asked.

Aunt Lucinda reached into her bejeweled purse and pulled out a compact mirror, which  she gladly held up for Mum to peer into.

"AH!" Mum yelped as she caught sight of her reflection. She scrambled to her feet. "Would you excuse me one moment?"

She ran full pelt out of the room toward the bathrooms. I put my head in my hands and wished desperately that this was all a crazy, mortifying, silly dream.

It wasn't.

"Well," Dad chuckled, leaning forward across the table and attempting to salvage the situation, "it's not every day you see someone with a big ice block on top of their head, eh, Mr. Mercury?"

My teacher shook his head slowly.

"No," he whispered. "It isn't."

"An ice-block gun?"

Mum laughed as I shook my head in disbelief at her explanation. We were driving home from my training session the next day. It had been completely exhausting, but I'd managed to spark beams from my hands, and light up the empty warehouse we'd been in, while controlling the energy blast. I'd only been able to do it for about three seconds, but Mum was overjoyed by my progress.

"This way," she'd said with a big grin on

her face, "you'll be able to light up a room without knocking people over at the same time. Which, you know, is always a good thing."

It may be a good thing, but it sucked all the energy out of me. I couldn't imagine being able to do it for a long period of time, but Mum said that came with practice, which was the whole point of these training lessons.

In the car on the way home, she took the opportunity to apologize for the disaster that was the parent-teacher evening, and revealed that she'd had to put a stop to an evil scientist in Yorkshire, who had invented an ice-block gun.

"Whatever he shoots at and hits gets turned to ice. He took a shot at me, but I ducked just in time. My hair wasn't quite so lucky, as you know. Anyway, I managed to put a stop to his evil plans to use it to take over the world, and handed him over to the police. He was planning on freezing the prime minister and her whole cabinet."

"Wow," I said, looking out of the window. "So, how did you know what he was up to?"

"You know I have my sources," she said, smiling mischievously. "As I promised, that side of things you'll learn a little later. Let's just get the basics under control for now."

In our training sessions, she had started to tell me a bit more about her day job and the sort of adventures she'd had in the past. So far, I'd heard stories about the Piano Prankster, who was so small and flexible that she could fit herself into grand pianos in which she'd hide during posh events held by public figures before jumping out in the middle of the speeches and holding everybody for ransom; the Blackout Burglar, who would cut the electricity supply to banks and jewelry shops before robbing them; the Silent Gymnast who stole thousands by using his gymnastic skills and an elaborate set of tools to raid London penthouses during the night without making a sound; and the Brunch Bandit who invited powerful politicians over for avocado on toast and then, when they went to the bathroom, she'd go through their bags and briefcases, learning a load of state secrets she could sell on the black market.

"What I don't get is how you managed to stop all these bad guys without the world finding out about your superpowers," I said, once she'd finished telling me all the details about the ice-block device.

"It's difficult," she nodded. "Luckily, nobody believes the criminals when they say that they were stopped by a woman who could create and control the power of light. I know I wouldn't believe them if I didn't know superpowers really do exist. Would you?"

"No." I hesitated, wondering whether I should ask the question on my mind, considering our family's current circumstances. I decided to just go for it.

"How did Dad find out about your superpowers?"

"Ah, well, that's an interesting story." She sighed, without looking at me and keeping her eyes on the road.

"We have the whole drive home for you to tell it."

She nodded.

"All right then. It was a long time ago on a lovely hot, sunny day in London and I'd just returned from saving the world from a particularly nasty character. She was a famous hypnotist, and was controlling some very powerful people without their knowledge. It had taken me days to work out how I was going to catch her in the act and stop her, but

I got there in the end. I was exhausted, so I decided to take a calming walk around Hyde Park, get myself an ice cream and sit on the grass and watch the world go by." She paused. "That was when I saw him."

She got this weird misty look in her eyes as she remembered.

"He was being chased around the park by a herd of angry alpacas which had escaped from London Zoo."

"WHAT?"

"I know." Her face broke into a grin. I felt a pang as I realized she hadn't smiled that broadly in a long time. "He was just running around yelling as this entire herd of alpacas zoomed along after him. I've never seen anything like it."

"Why was he being chased by alpacas?"

"They don't like lilac. It's a well-known fact in zoological circles. Alpacas absolutely cannot stand the color lilac. And what was your father wearing that day as he took a stroll through the park? A pair of lilac shorts. The alpacas were *furious*."

"So they attacked him?"

"They didn't get that far. As soon as I saw the chaos, I followed the herd and your father to a quieter corner of the park and used my power of energy to slow down the alpacas and keep them under control until the zookeepers arrived to take them back."

"Then what happened?"

"I broke the rules. Your father asked me how I managed to bring the alpacas under control and I was so enraptured by his honest  eyes and those silly lilac shorts, I told him the truth." She shrugged. "I told him I was a secret superhero. I just blurted it out, right there in Hyde Park, having kept this secret for years from everybody. My whole story just came tumbling out. And you know what he did?"

"Freaked out?"

"No, not at all. He didn't freak out; he didn't run away. He asked me if I'd like to go for waffles. So we did. And that was that."

She gave a sad smile.

"Hang on," I said. "Is that why in your wedding photos, Dad is wearing lilac shorts?"

She burst out laughing. "Yes! And to get to the ceremony, I had a carriage drawn by alpacas. He changed into lilac shorts for the wedding reception once the alpacas had safely left the vicinity."

"That's the true story, then? You didn't actually meet through friends, like you told us. You, in fact, met Dad while saving him from an angry herd of alpacas."

"Yes," she agreed, as we pulled into the driveway. "Your father knew the truth about me from the moment we met and loved me anyway."

She turned off the ignition and I could have sworn that her eyes suddenly filled with tears, but she cleared her throat and turned to look at me brightly, all trace of sadness in her expression vanished.

"Right, then, off you go. Great training session today and sorry again about the ice-block thing. I'll remember to check my appearance before I turn up at your school in the future."

"Do you want to come in and say hi to Dad?" I asked, hopefully. "You didn't get to talk much yesterday at the parent-teacher evening.

Dad's making baked potatoes for supper, one of your favorites. He told me this morning."

She paused as though considering it, but then shook her head.

"I had better not. I don't want to disturb your dinner."

I said goodbye and climbed out of the car, waving her off sadly. I don't know if it was the fact that I was super tired after my training session or whether the story about how she and Dad met had affected me somehow, but after Mum left that evening not even Dad pretending to waltz with Kimmy after dinner could cheer me up.

Over the next few days, I tried to forget about what was going on between Mum and Dad by throwing myself into learning to control my superpowers. It was an excellent distraction and every day I got better and better at controlling the intensity of the light I created from my hands. I was constantly distracted at school because I couldn't wait for lessons to finish, to get to the warehouse and shoot light beams all over the place. Nothing compared to that amazing tingly feeling that hurtled through me like lightning when I commanded my superpowers. I could make my whole body glow and fill the warehouse with a blinding white light on command.

It was *amazing*.

But the thing was, no matter how good it felt to have superpowers, I still felt sad.

Now that Mum had moved out, my training sessions were a nice opportunity to spend time with her, and I hated the afternoons when my phone would vibrate at school and it was

Mum canceling our training session because she had to "go stop a bad guy." The house felt weird without Mum and, even though he tried to pretend that everything was normal, I kept catching Dad looking really down. Alexis was shutting himself away in his room more than ever. I tried asking him if he was OK, but he told me he didn't want to talk about it and then he'd turn up the volume on his headphones, signaling my cue to leave.

"You OK about Mum and Dad, Clara?" I asked her, when we were playing with Kimmy in the garden one evening.

"I've been reading a book about parental separation in an attempt to develop greater understanding and empathy," she informed me, throwing the tennis ball across the grass and watching Kimmy race after it excitedly.

I smiled to myself. "What does it say?"

"That, as a family, we have to focus on self-awareness and be willing to challenge some of the ways in which we think about ourselves. We mustn't feel as though our parents are competing for our favor. It's all about good communication, understanding everyone's changing needs and meeting those needs as far as possible so that we can find the benefits in the situation for each individual."

"Right. Wow. And what do you think?"

Clara looked thoughtful as Kimmy dropped the ball back by her feet and wagged her tail eagerly. Clara picked up the ball and turned to face me, lifting her eyes to meet mine.

"I think it stinks," she sighed, throwing the ball high up into the air.

"Me too."

"At least Mum takes you to ballet almost every evening," she said. "I don't get to see her nearly as often."

We didn't say anything else about it, but

I hated knowing how sad Clara was. Aunt Lucinda wasn't making things easy either, constantly butting in on every family event, just like the parent-teacher evening. I still hadn't fully forgiven her for that and no amount of "but I was only looking out for you, darling" could make me forget the look on Suzie Bravo's face when, just as we were leaving, Alfred had attempted to peck at Mr. Mercury's head.

With my parents barely speaking, my aunt and her pet ostrich causing absolute chaos, and most of my spare time spent lighting up empty warehouses and parking lots, I couldn't wait for a day of normality at Kizzy's birthday party. I was excited to have a chance to forget about everything else going on and just have fun with my best friend.

But everything was about to get worse.

Kizzy could tell something was up.

In the week leading up to her birthday party, she kept saying how I wasn't spending any time with her after school anymore and mentioned how distracted I was in lessons. My homework was way behind and I had been doing badly in tests. I kept having to come up with lame excuses as to why I couldn't hang out with her whenever she suggested doing something nice together. She thought it was all connected with my parents' separation, which I guess was partly right, so she didn't have a go at me, even though I knew I kept letting her down. She just looked upset all the time.

I wished I could tell Kizzy everything about my superpowers. I knew she'd never tell a soul if I asked her not to – she's still never told anyone about that time she was sleeping over and I heard a weird noise, so I jumped out of bed and screamed, "WHAT DO YOU WANT, SCARY GHOST PERSON?!" and it turned out the noise was just her rolling over – but Mum had made me promise not to tell ANYONE about my superpowers. Not even my best friend.

And Kizzy wasn't the only one who picked up on something different about me. Ever since the parent-teacher evening, I'd noticed that I got a lot more stares at school and students whispered together when I passed them in the corridor. Mr. Mercury was on my case way more than before too, no doubt because my aunt's pet ostrich had pecked at his head and my mum had shown up to a meeting with him sporting an ice block instead of hair.

"Aurora Beam, if I catch you daydreaming one more time in my lesson, then I won't hesitate to give you extra homework, is that clear?" he threatened when he worked out I hadn't been listening to one word of his boring class. "Don't think that because your dad is giving us a fascinating exclusive tour of the Natural History Museum soon that you are above the law. I won't be showing favoritism."

"You're going to end up with detention if you're not careful," Kizzy pointed out the day before her party, as we sat in the canteen eating lunch. I didn't say anything, so she turned her attention to Suzie and Georgie who were sitting at the same table. Now that she couldn't spend as much time with me, I'd noticed that she'd been getting closer to their group.

"I'm excited about your birthday party tomorrow, Kizzy," Georgie smiled, sweeping her thick, glossy jet-black hair over one shoulder. "Thanks for inviting us."

"Have you got a good sound system?" Suzie asked, taking out her phone. "I have some great playlists that are perfect for routines."

"Routines?" Kizzy shot me a worried glance.

"Dance routines," Suzie explained. "I have been working on a new one that I thought I could teach everyone."

"Uh … OK!"

"Would you like me to bring my makeup suitcase? I could do everybody's face glitter if you wanted," Georgie suggested proudly.

"You have a makeup suitcase?" I asked, impressed.

"Duh, her mum gets sent it all for free

from the BEST brands," Suzie informed us. "Georgie is amazing at doing cool glitter patterns."

Georgie blushed at her friend's compliment. I had never really heard Suzie say anything nice about anyone, but then I guess I'd never spent that much time with her before now. Maybe she wasn't as horrible as I thought.

"I just pretend to know what I'm doing," Georgie laughed.

"I would really love that," Kizzy enthused. "I'm so excited that everybody's coming over. My dad is baking three types of cake. He tends to get carried away."

"I'm going to wear my new jeans," Suzie announced, standing up from the table to put her tray away. "Georgie personalized them for me. They look really good. Anyway, I've got to go and speak to Miss Nimble about my next gymnastics competition. I'll see you all later."

As she turned around to walk away, she suddenly let out such a piercing scream that Kizzy dropped her water glass and it spilled all over me and Georgie. I yelped and jumped up as the ice-cold water hit my lap, knocking into Mr. Mercury who at that moment had been passing behind me with his tray of food. His plate of spaghetti with tomato sauce slid down the tray as I bumped forcefully into it, landing with a loud **SPLAT** against his white shirt.

There was a collective gasp across the canteen.

"*Aurora. Beam*," Mr. Mercury hissed through gritted teeth, his face turning as red as the sauce dripping down his shirt.

"I'm s . . . so sorry," I gulped, barely able to get the words out. "I . . . uh . . . I . . ."

"It was my fault!" Kizzy said quickly. "I spilled water on her when Suzie screamed and it made her jump."

"And the reason I screamed is all Fred's fault!" Suzie snarled, as Fred Pepe sniggered next to her. "Look what he put on the floor right next to my shoe!"

We all turned to look at Fred, who shrugged and proudly opened his hand to reveal a fake dollop of dog poop.

"My bad," he said. "I got a new prank kit and knew I could get Suzie with it. But, I must say, this all turned out better than I could have imagined."

Mr. Mercury inhaled deeply with his eyes closed and I think I heard him counting to ten under his breath. When he opened his eyes, everybody in the room was watching him expectantly in utter silence.

"You are on your final warning, Miss Beam," he growled. "One more strike, and I'll not only give you detention for this term, I'll sign you up for the rest of your school career. Got it?"

I nodded.

"Good. For now, you can tell your parents they'll be receiving my dry-cleaning bill."

When I told Dad about the spaghetti incident that evening, he found it hilarious, but I didn't see what was so funny. After the mortifying experience of my aunt bringing along her deranged ostrich to a school event, I'd managed to draw even *more* attention to myself in front of the entire student population. And not in a good way.

So, the next day, I was looking forward to getting to Kizzy's party as soon as possible and proving to everyone in my class that I could function as a normal human being. Or at least pretend to.

"Are you on your way?" Kizzy asked hurriedly, when I picked up the phone.

"Almost," I assured her, sliding her present into my backpack. I'd gotten her a pretty bracelet, to match mine. After the way I'd been lately, I wanted to make sure she felt very special.

"I'm so nervous. What happens if no one turns up?"

"That's not going to happen. Suzie and Georgie said they were excited to come along, and if they're going to be there, then everyone else will be there too. Everyone loves you. Trust me, it will be the best party ever."

"And ... you're definitely coming?"

I paused midway through tying the laces of my Converse. "What do you mean?"

"It's just —" she hesitated "— it feels like you've been avoiding me recently."

"Kizzy, no, I—"

"I know you've got a lot going on with your parents and everything, but we never do things anymore. We don't hang out like we used to."

"That's only because—"

"And then I got you in even more trouble with Mr. Mercury and he already doesn't like you, so that doesn't help things."

"I don't—"

"So if you don't want to be best friends anymore, then—"

"KIZZY!" I cried, interrupting her. "You are my best friend in the whole world. Joint with Kimmy," I added, making her giggle. "I'm sorry, it's just... Well, I guess I've had a lot going on. And I don't care what grumpy Mr. Mercury thinks of me."

"OK," she said, sounding relieved. "And you promise you are coming to my birthday party? Because, remember, you promised you'd come to the cinema with me last week and I was waiting there on my own. . ."

"I'm so sorry about that, Kizzy," I said in my most sincere voice. "Like I said, something came up. . ."

I hoped she wouldn't push for what it actually was that had come up. I couldn't exactly tell her the truth: that I'd planned to meet her at the cinema after my training, but I was doing so well that Mum and I lost track of time, and when I looked at my watch, the movie had already finished. I still felt so bad whenever I pictured Kizzy standing on her own outside the cinema waiting for me to arrive.

"I know," she said. "But you promise nothing will come up today? You'll be there?"

"It's my best friend's birthday party. I'll be there."

I hung up, feeling terrible. I had to make it up to Kizzy, and making sure she had the best birthday ever would be a good start. I did a last-minute check in the mirror and then excitedly skipped across my room to my door and swung it open.

I screamed as, out of nowhere, a big orange beak came right at my face.

"Alfred!" I huffed, as he lifted his head and banged it on the lampshade hanging from the ceiling. "You have GOT to learn about personal space. Why are you here?"

"Oh, Aurora, thank goodness!"

Aunt Lucinda was hurrying up the stairs toward me, out of breath.

"We have to go," she said, grabbing my shoulders. "Now! Are you ready?"

"I don't need a lift to Kizzy's, she lives on this road," I informed her, checking my watch.

"What? What are you talking about?" She dropped her hands and looked at me strangely.

"Kizzy's birthday party. What are *you* talking about?"

"Oh, darling, you don't have time for that." She grabbed my hand and began to drag me down the stairs behind her. "We have an emergency."

"Aunt Lucinda," I said firmly, shaking my hand away as we got to the bottom and narrowly avoiding Alfred landing on top of my head as he slid down the bannister on his big feathered behind. "I can't have a day out with you today. It's my best friend's birthday party and I have to be there. I promised her."

"Aurora," she gasped, putting a hand on her heart and shaking her head at me. "Didn't you hear me? This is an emergency. It's one of the reasons I came back here from Bali; that's how important it is. I *need* you!"

"No offense, Aunt Lucinda, but needing to get last-minute reservations to a posh restaurant is not an emergency." I dodged past her to the front door. "I gotta go."

"Aurora, if I could, I would ask your mum to help, but she's busy sorting out another national crisis. This really is a world emergency and I can't do it alone, not with only my superpowers. I really need your help," she pleaded. "I'm afraid, whether we want it or not, we were given these superpowers for a reason."

There was something about her voice that made me stop in my tracks. I felt like she really needed me and I was being unreasonable. I knew she was talking sense and that I couldn't just ignore her.

She lifted her car keys and jangled them.

"We can go handle this and then I can drive you straight round to Kizzy's house for her birthday party."

"All right."

"Wonderful! I'll drop you at your friend's party afterward, I promise. Come on," she said, ushering me out the front door and toward her sports car, with Alfred following closely behind, now wearing one of Dad's raincoats that he'd stolen from the hooks by the door.

"I guess it is kind of exciting," I admitted, putting my seat belt on as she turned on the ignition. "My first superhero mission."

"And this one is VERY important, darling," she nodded, sharing a glance with Alfred in the rearview mirror. "Trust me."

11

"Are you sure this is it?" I asked nervously, peering down at Aunt Lucinda and Alfred from the air duct.

"Oh, yes," Aunt Lucinda replied, squeezing antibacterial hand gel onto her palms after having given me a leg up so I could remove the grate in the ceiling and climb in. "Thank goodness you're here! Alfred and I would never have fit in those air vents. Now, as I said, crawl straight that way and then take the first right, then the second left, then left again.

You'll happen upon a package – grab it and then come back here as quickly as possible."

I gulped and nodded, staring down the dark, cramped tunnel before me. I gave Aunt Lucinda a thumbs-up and began to shuffle forward on my hands and knees, repeating the directions in my head: *first right, second left, left again.*

Aunt Lucinda had been very vague about the package we had to rescue from this secret hiding place, no doubt trying to protect me from whatever horrible thing was in it. In the car on the way, she explained she'd received information that an evil criminal had hidden a package in the ceiling air vents above a famous London auction house years ago. The criminal was due for release from prison any day now and it was imperative to national security that he did not get his hands on this item.

"If we don't get there before he collects it —" Aunt Lucinda had whispered, her eyes welling up with tears of fear "— life as we know it will be changed forever."

We'd had to break into the back room of the auction house where there was an entrance to the air vents — Aunt Lucinda had come prepared with some blueprints of the building. She was right too, about fitting into these air vents; there was no chance she would have squeezed in. My spine was practically scratching along the top of the tunnel. I felt better knowing that I was helping to save the world, even though I didn't feel very brave as I crawled in the darkness.

The farther I went, the darker it became. I turned my palms upward and took a deep breath, pushing aside my fear about what this evil package might be, and calmly drew my focus to my powers, just as Mum had taught me. Bright beams immediately sparked from my fingertips, sending a powerful surge of light throughout the tunnel, so I could see where I was going. I smiled to myself. The training sessions really were working.

"Well done, Aurora!" I heard Aunt Lucinda cry from below me. She must have seen the

light glowing through the duct opening above her.

I ducked right as the air vent split into

separate pathways, then made
my way to the
second left.

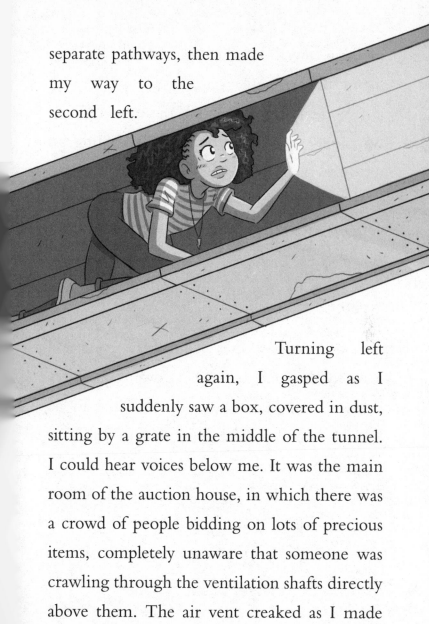

Turning left
again, I gasped as I
suddenly saw a box, covered in dust,
sitting by a grate in the middle of the tunnel.
I could hear voices below me. It was the main
room of the auction house, in which there was
a crowd of people bidding on lots of precious
items, completely unaware that someone was
crawling through the ventilation shafts directly
above them. The air vent creaked as I made

my way toward the package, making me stop in my tracks.

I suddenly had a vision of the tunnel giving way and me crashing through the ceiling on top of everyone. I bit my lip.

"Come on, Aurora," I whispered to myself as my heart thudded against my chest. "You can do this."

I carefully moved forward, ignoring the echo of another loud creak down the tunnel. As I got closer, I stretched out my hand and reached the box, pulling it toward me very slowly. Aunt Lucinda had warned me to be VERY careful with the box when I had it in my grasp, which wasn't exactly comforting. What *was* this thing? Clutching it in my fingers, I began to crawl backward because there was no room to turn around. I was so nervous about the package that my light began to ebb. I tried to pull my focus back, but I just couldn't. The tunnel fell into darkness. Had I gone right yet? Or was it left? Wait, I was getting confused. It was all the wrong way round. It suddenly felt very cramped and hot in here. I began to panic.

"Aurora?"

Aunt Lucinda's soft voice came echoing down the tunnel behind me.

"This way, Aurora! You can do it! I'm so proud of you!"

Feeling a boost of confidence from her encouragement and remembering that this was for the safety of others, my palms began to glow again. Not with the same power as before, but with a flickering of light. I continued shuffling backward, following the sound of Aunt Lucinda's voice until my legs fell through the hole of the ceiling where she was waiting for me. Alfred hurriedly moved under my dangling legs and Aunt Lucinda reached up to catch me under the arms and place me safely on the ground.

"Here," I breathed, holding out the box. "Got it."

"Well done!" Aunt Lucinda cried, eagerly snatching the box from my hands. "You've done very well."

She suddenly twisted the clasp and opened the lid of the box, making me instinctively duck and cover my head with my arms.

"What are you doing?" I yelped, crouched on the ground. "Are you mad?"

But she took no notice of me. Instead her eyes widened with delight and she presented the contents of the box for Alfred to see.

"At last. It's ours."

"Aunt Lucinda," I said slowly, straightening up. "What's going on?"

"What's going on is that I am now in possession of one of most priceless items on the planet." She lifted a sparkling necklace with a big blue diamond pendant from the box. "This is the Dream Diamond. Do you know how much this is worth?"

"But... I thought... You told me that this was an emergency! That the package was left there by an evil criminal?"

"It was, darling! Awful man," she sighed, unable to take her eyes off the diamond resting in her hand. "I helped him steal this years ago before he got caught and put in prison. I've been wondering all this time where he hid it and finally I was able to get it out of him. I should have known he'd hide it here. This is where we stole it from. He never was the most creative of thieves."

She smiled and put the necklace on, patting the diamond safely. Alfred peered at it closely and then hopped from side to side on his long ostrich legs in excitement.

"You have no idea how long I have waited to get my hands on what is rightfully mine," she beamed, tickling Alfred's chin. "Thank you, Aurora."

"Aunt Lucinda!" I stood frozen in shock. "You tricked me! You used that charm thing you can do, didn't you?"

"Of course I did. If I'd told you the truth you'd hardly have helped me, would you?" She rolled her eyes. "You get that streak of righteousness from your mother; it's very tiresome. I had to use my powers of persuasion on you. But still, I'm very impressed with *your* powers, Aurora." She looked at me carefully. "Kiyana hadn't mentioned how strong they were in you; it really is very strange for them to be showing themselves this young. I wonder what else you'll be able to do in time."

I clenched my fists. "You made me miss Kizzy's party to help you steal a priceless diamond! I thought I was saving the world! You had tears in your eyes! You betrayed me!"

"You'd have tears in your eyes too if you knew you were close to having this beauty around your neck! Plus, it's not stealing when it's rightfully yours. The only reason it ended up at the auction house is because my grandfather was silly enough to donate it out of the family decades ago," she said all defensively. "And don't be so dramatic – this was not a betrayal. This was a life lesson."

"In what? Trusting the wrong people?" I yelled.

"Don't shout, Aurora, someone will hear you," she hushed, glancing at the door that led to the main auction room. "A lesson in what you can do if you put your powers to good use. Nothing is out of your reach. Now," she smiled, getting the car keys out of her handbag, "we had better get going. Your little friend will be wondering where you are."

I was so angry, I couldn't even look at Aunt Lucinda for the entire drive, let alone speak to her. Not that she noticed; she was too busy admiring the diamond in her car mirrors every chance she got. I had five missed calls from Kizzy, two voice mails and about a hundred text messages asking where I was. By the time we got to our road, it was time for everyone to be picked up from the party.

"Don't be too angry with me, darling," Aunt Lucinda said as we drove up to Kizzy's house. "A love of jewels and gems is in our blood."

"What are you talking about?" I grumbled.

"Didn't Kiyana tell you? That's where all our superpowers come from in the first place." She pulled in to the side of the road. "Supposedly, anyway. Our ancestor, Dawn, found a mysterious stone buried in the darkness and that's how she returned light to the world. Of course, that's just the legend but—"

"Aunt Lucinda, I really don't have time for more ridiculous lies," I snapped, unbuckling my seat belt and getting out of the car, slamming the door behind me. "Please leave me alone."

"Well, there's no need to be like that." She chuckled as I walked away. "Have a lovely time! *Ciao*, darling!"

I heard her sports car zoom off as I ran down Kizzy's driveway and knocked loudly on the door. No one answered. I knocked again, for longer this time. Suddenly, it swung open and Georgie Taylor stood in the doorway, looking at me suspiciously. She had colored glitter perfectly swirled in a rainbow round her eyes.

"About time," she said, raising her eyebrows.

"Is Kizzy here? I need to speak to her."

"She doesn't want to talk to you."

"What?"

"Aurora," Georgie said, her expression softening, "she's kind of upset that you didn't show. Aren't you guys meant to be best friends?"

"I have a good reason. It was my aunt, she—"

"The party's over, Aurora, everyone has gone home except for us," came a voice behind Georgie. Suzie moved forward to stand next to her friend, folding her arms and looking down at me in superiority, with matching glitter around her eyes.

"I know it seems bad, but I have a good reason. Please can I talk to her?"

"She's busy," Suzie sighed, flicking her hair back. "We were in the middle of

a display. I've been perfecting my backflips."

I shared a glance with Georgie as Suzie pulled out a compact mirror from her pocket to check that her glitter was all intact. She snapped it shut.

"Better get back to it, she's waiting. Bye then," she said, attempting to shut the door by ushering Georgie out the way.

"Wait!" I pulled Kizzy's present from my bag. "Can you at least give her this?"

As I held out the present, Kizzy appeared, shuffling into the door frame between Georgie and Suzie. She had matching eye glitter too.

"Kizzy! Here, this is for you. Happy birthday!"

"Thanks," she mumbled, taking her gift.

"Kizzy, I'm so sorry, I—"

"It's OK, Aurora, I get it."

"No, you don't get it. You know what my aunt's like, she—"

"You didn't even call," she interrupted, her eyes full of hurt.

At this point, Suzie got bored and turned on her heel, walking back into the house. "Come on, Georgie," she said, disappearing down the hall. "We need to move Kizzy's furniture so we have space for the flips. I want to try something new for the next routine. My next competition is in a few weeks and backward somersaults are imperative to getting that perfect ten."

As Georgie followed her, leaving just us, Kizzy shook her head.

"Suzie completely took over everything," she whispered, glancing back to make sure they couldn't hear. Suzie's voice echoed through the house as she barked orders about where to move sofas before turning on some music for her routine.

"Kizzy," I began desperately.

"It was like it was her birthday party, not mine. We had to watch her routines all day. Still," she sighed, "at least she showed up. And Georgie has been really nice. She did everyone's glitter and she helped me decorate my backpack to match hers."

"Please, if you could just—"

"You're meant to be my best friend. Instead you're just shutting me out. It's like you don't want me around anymore."

"That's not true!" I protested. "I can explain."

"OK, then."

"Huh?"

"Explain," she said, watching me with curiosity. "Explain why you couldn't come today even though you promised this morning."

"I... Well ... I can't *exactly* explain but—"

"I knew it." She shook her head. "Another secret."

"I wish I could tell you, but I just can't! It's complicated. You wouldn't understand."

Her eyes filled with tears. "Well, maybe you should find a new best friend who can."

She shut the door gently, leaving me standing on her doorstep alone.

12

"And this is the staff canteen," my dad informed my class chirpily. "We eat lunch here! The sandwiches are *rad*."

Rad? Did he just say ... *rad*? No one has used the word "rad" since the ice age.

"When Aurora was little, we found her under one of these tables chatting away to a fossil that she'd stolen from a display," he chuckled, winking at me. "Naughty little munchkin!"

MUNCHKIN???

This. Could. Not. Get. Any. Worse.

When Mr. Mercury had mentioned at the beginning of term that he'd love to speak to my dad about organizing a school trip to the Natural History Museum, I was like, "Sure thing, Mr. Mercury," because I just thought, you know, he was a new teacher and he was being enthusiastic and I'd hit him on the head with that ball earlier that week, so I was trying to be nice.

And now here we were, on a behind-the-scenes tour directed by my dad, who was telling childhood stories and using words like "rad." Why had I done this to myself?!

As my dad continued to ruin my life, I glanced over at Suzie and Georgie, who were still giggling at the fossil story. Kizzy was with them, doing a very good job of looking interested in everything my dad was saying.

She still hadn't spoken to me since her party.

She spent all her time with Suzie and Georgie now and I had no one to partner with in group projects or in PE, and I had to sit on my own at lunch watching her laugh politely at whatever Suzie was saying and admire all of Georgie's must-have accessories. She and Georgie had those matching backpacks now too.

Since our falling-out, I hadn't been able to focus in my training sessions and Mum kept badgering me about what was going on until I exploded.

With words this time, rather than light beams.

"Maybe I don't want to have superpowers anymore!" I had yelled, when for the fourth time that week I hadn't been able to do anything.

"What do you mean?" Mum had asked, baffled.

"They've ruined everything. Dad was right. They make you forget what's important." I had picked up my bag and wiped away a tear. "I just want to go home."

She didn't say anything — she just nodded and drove me home, waiting until I went up to my room and shut the door before going to speak to Dad. Hearing Mum's voice, Clara had poked her head round my bedroom door.

"Is Mum downstairs?" she asked eagerly, coming into my room with a book tucked

under her arm.

I nodded. "She's not staying though."

"Oh."

I felt a pang at her crestfallen expression and patted my bed for her to come sit next to me.

"I miss her around the house too. And I've been a lousy big sister," I admitted as she climbed up and rested her head on my shoulder. "I'm sorry I haven't been around much in the evenings."

"Don't worry, you've been busy with your ballet lessons. You must be really good by now."

"I'm going to start making it up to you, and to everyone else now," I said firmly, speaking more to myself than to her. "Starting with no more ballet."

After that night, Mum didn't argue with me when I said I didn't want to do any more training and that I was giving up my superpowers. Instead, I went straight home after school and walked Kimmy with Dad and Clara or played computer games with Alexis, when he let me. And now that she wasn't teaching me every spare moment she had, Mum was able to take us all out more.

You know, when she wasn't busy saving the world.

Aunt Lucinda raised her eyebrows when I told her that my family and friends were more important than my superpowers, so I'd be focusing on just them from now on, but she didn't try and persuade me otherwise. She just clicked her tongue in disapproval, said I was missing out on a life of diamonds and VIP passes, and then asked if I'd be a darling and fetch more ice for her mojito.

I had learned my lesson and all I had to do now was make things right with Kizzy. The school trip to the Natural History Museum was the perfect opportunity to try and talk to her properly.

Dad led the class from the canteen down a load of stairs and through to the back rooms of the museum. Mr. Mercury, who was in charge of the trip, walked with him at the front, asking hundreds of intense questions and trying to encourage us all to ask questions too.

As they yabbered away about Dad's upcoming precious stones exhibition, I tried to catch up with Kizzy, standing directly behind her as Dad gathered us into a group ready to launch into a lecture on the mineralogical storage rooms before us.

That was when it started to happen.

One minute, I was feeling fine, building up the courage to tap Kizzy on her shoulder, and the next minute I felt that familiar warmth of tingles rushing down my arms and into my palms.

I shook my head; I must have been imagining it. I was in control of my powers now; this didn't happen anymore. Maybe it was withdrawal symptoms? I ignored it and focused on what exactly I was going to say to Kizzy.

But there it was again: a surge of warmth prickling through my body, all the way through to my fingertips. I bit my lip and glanced down at my hands.

The scar on my palm was *glowing*.

"Aurora, are you OK?" Kizzy whispered, as my dad droned on.

She had turned around and was watching me curiously, before she followed my gaze down to my hands. She gasped.

I couldn't risk it, I had to get out of there before something happened. Without responding to Kizzy, I spun round and pushed through the group to the back, racing down the corridor and around the corner, ducking through the first door I came to and slamming it shut behind me.

I was in a dark storage room with aisles of neatly labeled and locked drawers. I hadn't been in there for years, but I recognized it from when Dad took Alexis, Clara and me to work one day. It was one of the back rooms that stored all the collections that weren't due to go on display for the public yet. I remembered Dad proudly showing us the vaults at the back of the room that contained all the artifacts that he was responsible for preserving and organizing.

Luckily, I was on my own. My hands now felt like they were burning with heat; I had no idea what was happening. The sparkling glow from the scar on my palm had brightened and spread, so that my hands were lit up too.

"Stop it!" I instructed my hands to no avail. "Stop doing that!"

"Aurora?"

I screamed as Fred Pepe appeared from among the boxes.

"Fred, what are you doing in here?" I cried, hiding my hands behind my back.

"I got bored with your dad talking about sandwiches, no offense, so I thought I'd go exploring. They have some pretty cool ancient stuff in these back rooms. You should see the animal skeletons." He waved a bone in his hand triumphantly. "This is from a whale! I know we're not supposed to take stuff but I thought I could borrow... Wait, Aurora, are you ... *glowing*?"

The door burst open behind me, as Kizzy ran through.

"There you are!" she said, catching her breath.

Georgie and Suzie rushed in after her, shutting the door behind them.

"You brought *them*?" I hissed at Kizzy, stumbling backward as I desperately tried to hide the light emanating from me.

"We followed," Georgie answered, folding her arms. "What's going on?"

"Great idea to escape, Kizzy. That talk was SUCH a yawn. Why can't we ever do cool school trips, like to a musical or something? Who cares about dinosaurs and weird old rocks?" Suzie stopped when she saw me and Fred. "Hey... What are you guys doing in here?"

"Aurora," Kizzy said, looking frightened. "What's happening to you?"

My hands grew hotter and hotter. I just about managed to yell, "DUCK!" as energy burst from my palms and a blinding white light filled the room. After a few seconds, it took all my concentration to bring the sparks under control, plummeting us back into the dim of the ceiling strip lights and leaving my scar with a warm glow.

There was a loud thud as Suzie fainted, landing next to where Georgie and Kizzy were crouched, staring up at me with their mouths wide open in shock.

The bone Fred was holding dropped from his hand, clattering loudly on the floor.

"Aurora, I speak for everyone when I say –" he began, a wide grin spreading across his face – "that was AWESOME."

13

Mr. Mercury gave us detention.

By the time he came barging into the room, after hearing the commotion and realizing some students were missing, Georgie and Kizzy had helped Suzie to her feet and I'd begged them not to tell anyone what they'd just witnessed. Due to the sheer force of my powers, all the boxes and shelves had been knocked to the ground and were scattered everywhere. Just like our still-recovering garden, the room looked as though it had been hit by a tornado.

I hadn't sent out that kind of energy beam for ages.

Mr. Mercury gasped as he took in the chaos. "What happened in here?"

Dad, who had come running in behind Mr. Mercury, took one look at the disaster zone and instantly turned to me. He knew EXACTLY what had happened.

"Ah, that . . . uh. . . . That silly air-conditioning unit," Dad said hurriedly, with a nervous laugh.

Everyone turned to look at him.

"Must get that fixed."

Mr. Mercury looked at him like he had lost his marbles. "*Air-conditioning* did this?"

"Yes, and may it be a lesson to you all to check your air-conditioning units and make sure they are in good working order. I think I've got some interns in next week, so clearing this up should be a fun job for them. Anyone hurt? No? Fantastic. Let's move on to the next part of the tour, shall we?"

"But, Professor Beam," Mr. Mercury hesitated, still casting his eyes over the damage, "all the items in here... Shouldn't we check that everything is in order for your exhibitions?"

"Nah, I wouldn't bother," Dad said, in a much higher-pitched tone than normal. "All of this is mostly my notes and a few historical antiquities that we don't include in the main exhibitions. The most valuable items preserved for my displays are in those vaults at the back, and, trust me, nothing can get in or out of those. They are heavily secured."

Mr. Mercury nodded slowly before turning to look accusingly at us.

"What were you all doing in here?"

The five of us stared blankly at him. I tried desperately to make my brain function and come up with an excuse but I was distracted by trying to keep my glowing hands out of sight. My fingertips were still tingling and I didn't feel in control.

"*Well*?" Mr. Mercury's face was growing redder and redder as none of us spoke.

"Whale bone," Fred blurted out.

"Excuse me?"

"Whale bone," Fred repeated, casting his eyes across the mess surrounding him. "Aha! Here it is."

He bent down and pulled the whale bone he'd had earlier from underneath a pile of books and old coins that had spilled from their box. He passed it to Dad.

"You were in here looking for ... a whale bone?" Mr. Mercury asked, his brow furrowed in confusion.

"Yes, that's right," Georgie chipped in confidently. "We heard it was missing and we thought we might put ourselves to use. You are welcome, Professor Beam."

"But, who said to—"

"Excellent work, team!" Dad enthused, catching on. "This whale bone is critical to the ... well, the whale bone display! Your students have been very helpful, Mr. Mercury."

"Well," Mr. Mercury said gruffly, "I don't care how helpful they've been, they shouldn't be snooping around a museum with valuable artifacts that don't belong to them!"

"We would never steal," Georgie said, looking insulted.

"Yeah! And if we did steal any whale bones, we'd bring them back in a few weeks or whatever, so it's more like borrowing anyway," Fred added indignantly before Georgie shushed him.

"Well, none of you should have gone anywhere in this museum without my permission," Mr. Mercury scolded. "Detention tomorrow for all of you."

"I don't feel well," I said suddenly. The tingles in my fingertips were growing warmer and warmer. "I have to get out."

Mr. Mercury narrowed his eyes at me suspiciously, but thankfully didn't ask any more questions. He begrudgingly said he'd take me outside, but Dad insisted on it, asking one of his colleagues to continue with the tour and encouraging Mr. Mercury to guide the others back to the group. As soon as Dad and I got to the top of the stairs and stepped outside through the emergency exit, a wave of crisp, fresh air hit me and I felt instantly better.

"I'm so sorry," I said, breathing heavily and sitting down on the pavement.

"What happened?" Dad asked, sitting down next to me with a concerned expression.

"I don't know! My powers. I couldn't control

them. It was like that time with Clara and the bullies. Or the garden. Except, more intense. I can't explain it." I sighed. "Dad, I'm so sorry about ruining the storeroom. I feel terrible."

"Don't worry about it. Let's get you home."

Mum was pacing up and down the driveway when we got home and threw her arms around me as soon as I stepped out of the car. Dad must have called her when I was waiting for him to get his stuff from the office. She led me to the sofa while Dad put the kettle on. Kimmy came running from her bed and leapt up onto my lap, licking my face.

"Tell me exactly what happened," Mum instructed, gently pulling Kimmy down.

So I did. She sat and listened while I went through it all, nodding patiently and not saying anything until I was finished. Dad put the hot chocolate down in front of us, and settled back into the sofa opposite with his mug.

"And you had no control whatsoever?"

"None." I took a deep breath. "Mum, it was really scary."

"It's OK." She smiled, placing a hand over mine. "You've got a lot on your plate; it must have just ... spilled over into your powers somehow."

I shook my head. "That's not it. Something triggered it."

"I've been meaning to speak to you, Aurora." Mum lowered her eyes. "I wanted to apologize for putting too much pressure on you. For making you work so hard. Especially with everything else that's going on. It's my fault this happened."

"It's not your fault," Dad protested. "And if it is, then it's just as much mine."

Mum smiled at him gratefully and then took a sip of her hot chocolate.

"You've put hazelnut syrup in it!" she enthused.

"Your favorite." Dad blushed. "I always thought you were just making it up but ... I decided to give it a try recently and you're right, it is an excellent addition."

I glanced from Mum to Dad and back to Mum again.

It was a really nice moment and everything, don't get me wrong, but HELLO I just almost blew up the *Natural History Museum*! This was not the time to discuss hazelnut syrup.

I tried to explain to them that this time there was something different, but Mum was convinced that it was an "emotional overload"

from all the pressures I was under and Dad agreed. I gave in and went to bed early to try and "get some rest," but how could I? All I could think about was the fact that I couldn't control the superpowers. Something happened to me in the museum and I didn't know what. What about my scar? Why did it glow like that and why did it feel raw now, like a fresh cut on my palm, when I was born with it? And what was I supposed to say to Kizzy and the others? They had literally *seen* light beams come out of my hands. There was no way I could make up anything that would explain the incident away.

The first tactic I attempted was to just avoid the four witnesses the next day. I was doing quite well – purposefully averting their pointed looks in lessons and hiding in the theater props room at break times – until Mr. Mercury reminded me about detention when his class finished at the end of the day and I tried to make a break for it.

I said I wasn't feeling too good, like on the school trip, but he just raised his eyebrows at me and said, "Anyone who is well enough to eat two helpings of dessert, is well enough to sit through detention."

Which is not true because sick people always eat ice cream.

But even when I made that point, he just waved his hand impatiently at me to leave him alone and sit back down. Suzie, Georgie, Kizzy and Fred were all staring at me as I sat down on the opposite side of the room to them. I pretended like I didn't notice and just got out my homework, flicking through my textbook all innocently.

"OK, I'll be five minutes," Mr. Mercury yawned a few minutes in, scraping his chair back and standing up.

"Wait! What?" I squeaked, knowing that as soon as I was left alone with them, I'd receive a barrage of questions. "Where are you going?"

"To the men's room," Mr. Mercury replied, looking at me strangely. "If that's all right with you?"

"Are you sure you can't hold it? I know they say it's bad for the bladder, but what do they know?"

WHY WAS I TALKING ABOUT BLADDERS?

Mr. Mercury blinked at me. "No, Miss Beam, I can't hold it. Not that it's any of your business. And it is, in fact, bad for your bladder. Now, back to work before I give you a week's worth of detention for being cheeky."

He left the room, shaking his head and muttering something about strange students at this school.

"So," Fred said, as I pretended to be

busy, "you want to explain what happened yesterday?"

"You've been avoiding us all day," Kizzy remarked.

"What? No, I haven't!" I laughed breezily.

"Oh really?" she said with a hint of a smile. "You weren't hiding in the theater props room at lunchtime?"

"Wait, how did you know?"

"I've known you forever."

"That's not the important point here," Georgie pointed out. "The question is, what happened? We have a right to know."

Suzie narrowed her eyes at me. "Are you an alien?"

"What? No! Why would you think I was an alien?"

"Because you began to glow and then all these sparks flew out of your fingertips and suddenly the room was filled with a burst of light, like a flash of lightning, blinding us all momentarily," Fred explained. "Suzie thought you might be an alien. I reckon it's a science experiment gone wrong, especially as your dad is a professor."

I held up my hands and Suzie flinched.

"I'm not an alien or a science experiment gone wrong. Just forget it, OK?"

Fred shook his head. "Nope, you're not getting away that easy. What's going on?"

"Can't we just leave it? We have a lot of homework to do. It was nothing!"

"Aurora, what we saw wasn't nothing," Kizzy said quietly. "Please tell us."

I sighed and closed my eyes. I knew they weren't going to leave it alone. I thought about coming up with some kind of excuse, but there was nothing that would fully explain the museum incident, except for the truth. They had seen my hands glowing and they had seen the light beams shoot out of them.

"Fine." I took a deep breath. "I kind of have ... superpowers."

There was a stunned silence before Fred whooped and fist pumped the air. Suzie picked up her science textbook and began to fan herself with it.

"This is SO COOL!" Fred exclaimed, jumping up and down in his seat. "So, you're a superhero? I knew it!"

"No!"

"I can't believe this!" Kizzy whispered. "*Superpowers?*"

"I know it sounds unbelievable but—"

"We all saw it," Fred nodded eagerly. "So we believe it all right."

"Please forget what you saw."

"Like that's going to happen any time soon," Fred snorted, looking at me in admiration. "So, what sort of thing can you do? Are you superfast? Superstrong? Can you turn invisible? Can you fly? Can you read minds? Like, what am I thinking right now?"

"No, nothing like that! Just the light beams. But, please, you have to promise not to tell anyone," I pleaded. "It's really important no one else finds out."

"This is just like a Marvel or DC movie," Fred said, his eyes wide with excitement.

"No, it's not. I'm not a superhero and I'm never going to be. What you saw was a one-time thing and it's never going to happen again. Promise me you won't tell anyone?"

Before anyone could reply, the door swung open and Mr. Mercury came back into the room.

"No more noise," he barked, sitting down at his desk and picking up his book. "Back to work."

I turned my attention back to my textbook and tried to hide my face as my eyes filled with tears.

My secret was out.

14

For the rest of that week, I felt more alone than ever.

I kept seeing Kizzy, Georgie, Suzie and Fred huddled together, whispering and glancing over. I knew they were talking about me and, knowing Suzie, likely saying bad things, so I avoided them, even when Kizzy tried approaching me a few times. Despite me having said very clearly in detention that I had given up my powers, the fact that they knew about them made me a freak in their eyes. Plus, they'd seen what came over me in the museum, so they could hardly trust me to keep control of my powers around them. I kept waiting for Suzie to tell someone and for me to be expelled on the spot. No parent would want someone like me around their children.

Plus, Mum's absence from the house seemed even more noticeable these days, because usually when she was "working late," Dad would be around, but, thanks to the big exhibition launch coming up, he was staying late at the museum most evenings. Then Dad made things worse, by asking Aunt Lucinda to pick us up from school and drop us home on the days he couldn't make it in time. I tried to argue against this disastrous decision, reminding him what she was like, but he insisted that she was the only person he could ask at such late notice.

"Where's Mum?" Alexis grumbled one

evening from the front seat, as Aunt Lucinda explained that Dad was stuck at work, and Clara and I attempted to squeeze in next to Alfred.

You have never experienced a truly uncomfortable car journey until you have sat in the back seat of a sports car with a grumpy ostrich.

They have a very wide gait.

"An evil genius is trying to take over the world from an island off Scotland using a rocket launcher," she explained, checking her lipstick in the mirror, while I froze. "Your mum's had to pop up to stop him."

What on earth was she thinking telling them the TRUTH?! Had she lost her mind?!

"Sure," Alexis sighed, "so she's stuck in a boardroom meeting then. Remind me never to get an office job when I'm older. The hours suck."

I breathed a sigh of relief as Aunt Lucinda caught my eye in the side mirror and winked. While we all waited patiently in the car for her to do her lip liner, Clara decided to pass the time by giving Alfred's wing a friendly scratch. Unfortunately, her gesture of kindness toward him backfired as he began to thump his leg, just like Kimmy does when you get the right tickle spot on her belly, which is really cute.

But ostrich legs are much bigger and more powerful than dog legs, and when Alfred started kicking his leg clumsily in appreciation at the scratch, his foot slammed right down and dented the floor of the car. Clara immediately stopped scratching his wing and looked from the big dent in the car to me guiltily. I put a finger to my lips, nodding at a completely unaware Aunt Lucinda, still perfecting the outline of her lips. Clara giggled.

"There's that boring bald teacher of yours," Aunt Lucinda said, tearing her gaze from her own reflection. "I think he's coming over to say hello. Helloooooooo!"

She wiggled her fingers at Mr. Mercury, who was walking out of school with a pile of marking to do. He winced when he saw her and I sank lower into my seat.

"Ah ... hello, Ms. Beam. Nice to see you again. And your ... um ... pet."

Alfred ruffled his feathers and looked Mr. Mercury up and down with his large, beady eyes.

"And you, Mr. Jupiter!"

"It's Mr. Mercury," I hissed, my cheeks burning.

"I hear the Natural History Museum trip was quite the success," she continued, ignoring me. "Very heroic of you to take the children. I couldn't handle so many of them running about."

"Well, it is my job, I suppose," he replied, standing by the car awkwardly. His eyes suddenly bulged out of his head as he spotted the blue diamond round her neck. "That's a very pretty necklace."

"So sweet of you to notice!"

I rolled my eyes. You could hardly miss it.

"Is that the Dream Diamond?"

"It is! How refreshing to meet someone who appreciates fine things." She fluttered her eyelashes at him and Alexis glanced back at me in horror.

Was Aunt Lucinda FLIRTING with Mr. Mercury?

Kill me now. Kill me now. Kill me now. Kill me now. Kill me now. Kill me n—

"I don't know much about it, I'm afraid. Only that the properties of that particular diamond are really quite fascinating. I'm a science teacher, you see." He blushed.

Mr. Mercury BLUSHED. AT AUNT LUCINDA.

This was worse than when Mum showed up at parents' evening with an ice block on her head.

"I'd love to hear all about its properties. Perhaps you could tell me over dinner?" Aunt Lucinda practically purred.

AHHHHHHHHHHHHHHHHHH-HHHHHHHHHHHHH!!!!

"Um... I ... well I..."

A flush of red rose from his cheeks all the

way over Mr. Mercury's bald head.

Even the top of his head was blushing.

"W ... won't I see you at the stone?" he finally managed to say. "I mean, launch! I mean, stone launch. Precious stone launch. At the museum? I assume you'll be wearing it then?"

"You're going to the launch?" Aunt Lucinda blinked at him in surprise.

"I know, it seems silly that I got an invitation to such a prestigious launch; me, just a lowly science teacher," he mumbled, jostling the books in his arms. "But I was telling Professor

Beam on the school trip to the museum how fascinated I was by those priceless stones, and he was kind enough to offer me an invitation. I'm very unprepared for that sort of thing; I'll have to track down a tuxedo!"

Brilliant. Thanks, Dad. Invite my TEACHER to your big event. Not that that is as embarrassing as my aunt inviting that same teacher on a date. Or the ice-block thing with Mum.

Seriously, what is wrong with my family?

Mr. Mercury must have been thinking the same thing as he suddenly cleared his throat nervously and asked in this high-pitched voice, "Will *all* the Beams be there?"

"Oh yes, we're all going," she confirmed, nodding. "It's a family affair!"

"Ah, how – " he searched for the word "– lovely."

"Of course! Well, I look forward to seeing you there, then." Aunt Lucinda smiled, flashing her pearly white teeth framed perfectly by her freshly applied red lipstick. "I'll wear the diamond and you can tell me all about it properly."

Mr. Mercury gulped. I genuinely felt sorry for him, despite the fact that he (a) gave me detention, (b) yells at me any chance he gets, and (c) hates me.

As I literally tried to bury myself in Alfred's feathers – who promptly wiggled his bum to bump me back out of them – Aunt Lucinda turned on the ignition and flicked her designer sunglasses from where they were resting on the top of her perfectly coiffed hair down onto her nose.

"Toodle-loo, Mr. Neptune!" She waved, before putting her foot down and speeding away from him.

Her exchange with my teacher, on top of everything else going on, had made school practically IMPOSSIBLE for the next few days because every time I sat in his class I couldn't make eye contact with him. I think he felt the same way because every now and then in his lessons I'd catch him staring at me, but then he'd look away really fast. I had never looked forward to a weekend more. I just wanted to lock myself in my room and be invisible.

On Saturday, Dad was at the museum putting together the finishing touches, so Mum took us out to a café for a big breakfast. Clara filled her in on all the new projects she was working on at school, while Alexis explained why he'd decided it would be a good idea to try and hack into a video-game company's software. Dad had been sent a strict warning from the company's lawyers.

"I was trying to get to the next level," he shrugged, with a mouthful of waffle.

"Can't you just play the video game, like

everyone else does?" Mum asked, passing him more syrup.

"Where's the fun in that?"

Mum shook her head at him sternly, but I noticed that when he turned away, a smile crept across her lips like she was secretly proud. Her phone rang just as she finished paying the bill and she excused herself to take the call, before returning to the table with a worried expression on her face.

"That was the office," she explained, giving me a knowing look. "I have to go."

"We understand," I said quickly before the other two could protest. "We can walk home, it's not far."

She nodded gratefully before giving us each a kiss, grabbing her coat and racing out so fast, that she became almost a blur. Alexis raised his eyebrows as she disappeared around the corner.

"Anyone else ever noticed that Mum is weirdly

fast? It's almost like she's got superpowers."

"Ha ha, good one, Alexis! So funny, *what a comedian!*" I replied, maybe a little too enthusiastically judging by the shocked reaction on both of their faces. I quickly changed the conversation by asking Clara to explain her caterpillar project to me again, but noticed Alexis watching me curiously on the walk home.

"Strange how Mum never talks about her job," he commented suddenly. "Dad won't shut up about his."

"Mum's is a boring office job whereas Dad's is quite cool," I reasoned. "Well, I'm not sure weird ancient stones are cool. But, you know, his is an unusual job."

Alexis didn't look convinced, but thankfully he didn't say anything else. I felt guilty about lying to him and Clara, but there was nothing I could do. When we got home, he shut himself up in his room and Clara went to read her book, so I was left on my own with Kimmy downstairs. I sat on the sofa and let her jump up to sit next to me.

"I wish that everything was back to normal, Kimmy," I admitted.

She looked at me with her large, pointy ears up and placed her right paw on my lap in solidarity.

"I can't talk to my brother and sister because it's all a big secret."

She tilted her head.

"And most people at school don't know the truth and the ones that do think I'm a big weirdo."

She tilted her head to the other side.

"And Mum and Dad are sad all the time because they've separated."

She leaned forward and nudged my nose with hers.

"But they're both too busy to make it better

again."

She inhaled deeply.

"Plus, my aunt asked my teacher out on a date just in case I wasn't already the biggest freak in school."

She exhaled deeply.

"I feel like no one understands and I have no one to talk to."

She barked.

"Apart from you, Kimmy, of course," I laughed, leaning forward to give her a hug and bury my face in her fur.

As she nuzzled my neck, the doorbell rang, making her immediately jump down and rush to the door.

"I'll get it!" I yelled up to Alexis and Clara, dragging myself off the sofa.

I pulled Kimmy back and opened the door. Standing on my doorstep were Fred, Suzie, Georgie and Kizzy.

"W ... what are you guys doing here?" I stammered as Kimmy barged past me to greet Kizzy with a big lick on the chin. It had been a while since she'd seen her.

"You've been avoiding us again," Kizzy laughed, stroking Kimmy's ears. "So we thought we'd come to you."

"Look, you don't need to worry," I said in a hushed tone. "I know you think I'm this big freak and I promise I—"

"Why would we think that?" Georgie asked, coming forward to pat Kimmy on the head.

"Because ... because of ... what I told you," I explained, wondering if she'd had a knock on the head recently and somehow forgotten everything.

"We don't think you're a freak," Kizzy said sternly.

"I do," Suzie muttered under her breath

before receiving a sharp jab in the ribs from Georgie. "Ow! Not a freak in a *bad* way."

Georgie smiled and rolled her eyes at her friend. "We wanted to tell you that we won't be telling anyone anything. Your secret is safe with us."

"It . . . it is?"

"Sure."

"Thanks. That's really nice of you."

"Whatever, this is the coolest thing that has EVER happened to me," Fred said. "I can't believe we're friends with a superhero."

"You want to be friends with me?" I asked in disbelief.

"Why else do you think we're here?" Georgie laughed. "We're in this together now."

"We couldn't let you deal with this on your own," Kizzy informed me stubbornly. "No wonder you've been distant lately."

"I'm so sorry, Kizzy, I didn't want to keep

letting you down. I've just had so much on my mind and I couldn't talk about it."

"You can now," Fred insisted. "Because we've formed a superhero club."

"You've WHAT?"

"A superhero club," Suzie repeated, flicking her hair behind her shoulders. "It's clear that you need a *lot* of help."

"Wait, what do you mean a *superhero club*?"

"What did you think we were going to do?" Suzie raised her eyebrows. "Sit back and let you mess up everything? The world doesn't stand a chance with people like you protecting it from bad guys. No offense."

"What Suzie is trying to say in her own way —" Georgie laughed "— is that we want to help."

"We've all got our own roles to play in the club, you know, should evil strike," Fred informed me, with a serious expression. "Suzie is going to help you with movement and gymnastics—"

"It's a necessary skill for a superhero to have," she said pompously.

"Georgie is going to help with your superhero costume."

"I have some *great* ideas for accessories." Georgie smiled.

"Kizzy is in charge of research, and will be the brains of the operation."

"I'll just help where I can." Kizzy blushed modestly.

"And I'm president of the club and simply a genuine genius," Fred concluded.

"Who made you president?" Suzie huffed.

"The club was MY idea. Naturally, that makes me president."

"Wait a second," I said quickly as Suzie opened her mouth to argue back. "I told you guys that I'm giving up my superpowers."

"Yeah, you said that, but the thing is," Kizzy smiled up at me, "you can't really stop being who you are."

"So, we're all agreed on superhero club then?" Fred asked as the others all nodded. "Good, we'll think of a name later. Shall we give her the gift now?"

Georgie opened her backpack and pulled out a box, handing it to me.

"What's this?"

"Duh," Suzie sighed. "Open it and see."

I lifted the lid of the box and inside were the coolest pair of sneakers I've ever seen. They were multicolored, with silver glitter toes, and as I lifted them out, I saw that on the heel of one it said "Lightning" sewn on in glitter letters and on the other, "Girl."

"They're the latest ones," Georgie said quickly, scrutinizing my face for a reaction. "My mum works with the brand."

"Georgie personalized them, though, so they're much better now." Kizzy grinned as I traced the letters of *Lightning Girl* with my finger. "It's the start of your costume."

"Every superhero has a costume," Fred said knowingly, "and every superhero has to have a superhero name. Kizzy came up with it and we all agreed it suited you and your powers perfectly."

"I came up with the name, but the sneakers were all Suzie's idea in the first place," Kizzy said.

"Very thoughtful, don't you think?"

"Whatever. You can't be a superhero in the kind of shoes you wear," Suzie sighed. "Again, no offense."

"Do you like them?" Georgie asked hopefully.

"Do you like the name?" Kizzy added nervously.

I didn't know what to say. I just stared at them, my eyes welling up with tears of gratitude.

"Let's take that as a yes all round," Suzie decided. "Can we come in now? I'm getting kind of cold and Kizzy said you make a good hot chocolate. With walnuts or something weird."

"Hazelnut," Georgie corrected, following Suzie past me through to the kitchen.

"I'll get things ready for the first superhero club meeting," Fred said, filing after Georgie, with Kimmy trotting in behind him. "Your dog can be part of the club too."

Kimmy licked his hand in agreement.

"Thanks so much, Kizzy," I said softly, putting the sneakers carefully back into their box. "I'm so happy we're friends again."

"Like Georgie said, you're not in this alone anymore. We're in it together."

She gave me a hug and we went into the kitchen where the others were all laughing at Kimmy dropping her slimy tennis ball into Suzie's lap, causing Suzie to scream at all the slobber.

"Every superhero needs a sidekick," Kizzy whispered to me with a smile. "Or five."

Dad's precious stone exhibition launch was a lot more posh than I thought it would be. Everyone was dressed in black tie and there were all these colored spotlights round the main gallery of the museum, making it feel like a Hollywood party. There was even a violin quartet, and lots of waiters strolling round topping up champagne glasses. The precious stones were on display on a plush purple velvet cushion in a big, thick glass cabinet right in the middle, with a red rope cordoning it off so you couldn't get too close.

Who knew that a bunch of weird rocks could cause such a party?

Dad was really in his element too, standing by the cabinet in his bright-red bow tie with his chest all puffed out like a proud peacock, greeting anyone who wandered over with a long lecture about their discovery. In the end, I was glad I'd listened to Aunt Lucinda when she told me that sneakers weren't appropriate for this kind of event, no matter how glittery and amazing they were. I put them in my bag though, just in case the shoes Georgie lent me to go with my long green dress started rubbing.

Even though Aunt Lucinda was right about the sneakers, I'm not sure I should be taking fashion advice from someone who thinks it's appropriate to wear a bright-pink ruffled ball gown wider than a car. When she came to pick us up – Mum was meeting us at the museum and Dad had to be early to make sure everything was in order – Kimmy was so freaked out by Aunt Lucinda's getup that she would not stop barking at her, and then when Kimmy approached the dress *very* carefully to check it out, she genuinely got lost in all the ruffles and couldn't find her way out again for two minutes.

It was lucky that Kizzy had been there helping me get ready since we needed the extra muscle to pack Aunt Lucinda into the taxi.

In the end we had to order two taxis as Alexis, Clara and I couldn't fit in with Lucinda's dress AND Alfred. I'm not sure how happy the taxi driver was at first about having an ostrich in his car, but considering Alfred was wearing a top hat, monocle and bow tie, he soon realized that he wasn't your average ostrich and let it go.

"I wish you could come," I said to Kizzy, slightly out of breath from shoehorning Aunt Lucinda into the car.

"Me too. But I'm excited to get going with all these." She gestured to the box of files on the ground next to her that she was taking home.

Once I'd explained to Mum that the superhero club knew the truth thanks to the school trip, she allowed me to swear them to secrecy and fill them in on her real job of saving the world. Georgie sat there in amazement, Fred almost passed out on the spot from excitement and Suzie remarked, "Well, that explains the ice-block hat, I suppose."

And when Kizzy got over the shock of that particular reveal, she begged my mum for permission to look into her previous cases. She was totally fascinated by Mum's secret life, plus she thought it would be excellent research for the superhero club. "You know," she said eagerly to Mum, who was listening to her with this bemused expression, "to learn about what Aurora might be up against in the future."

Mum eventually caved and let her take home all the files and newspaper clippings she'd collected over the years detailing her previous adventures.

"How come you never get caught?" Kizzy had asked, her eyes as wide as saucers.

"It's an art," Mum had chuckled. "The bad guys know who I am, but of course the police never believe them when they say someone with light beams shooting out of their hands had gotten in the way of their evil plans."

Kizzy was so excited about reading through Mum's files, that she'd invited the rest of the superhero club over to her house that evening for pizza to discuss her findings. "Don't worry," she assured me as I slid into the taxi next to Alexis, "I'll call you if I find anything really interesting."

It was only when I got to the museum that I realized I'd forgotten to tell her that no phones were allowed into the exhibition, to stop any unauthorized photos of the artifacts being taken. I put my phone in a labeled bag and reluctantly handed it to a security man at the door. Kizzy would have to wait until tomorrow to tell me all the weird, and likely embarrassing, stories she was going to discover about my mum.

Her eighties hairstyle alone is a story in

itself. Trust me, I've seen photos.

I'd much rather have been at Kizzy's house eating pizza with my new friends than standing awkwardly in the corner of a big glamorous party at the Natural History Museum. Apart from Alexis and Clara, I didn't have anyone to talk to, and frankly they were no use at all. As soon as we arrived, Alexis started his mission to snaffle as many canapés as possible, so I lost him in the crowd. Clara sneaked off to the cloakroom at the first chance she got, to read her book under the coats. I stood at the back with Alfred for a bit, but then he also left me, to size up to the ostrich skeleton standing in the Large Birds of Africa section. Thankfully I couldn't see Mr.

Mercury anywhere; I was hoping to avoid him the whole night. He was probably thinking the same thing about Aunt Lucinda, who was busy parting the crowds as she cheerfully made her way through to the champagne bar set up at the side of the gallery. At least she was easy to spot and he could ensure he was on the opposite side of the room at all times.

I helped myself to a sparkling elderflower drink and went to admire one of the stands that had been set up alongside the main cabinet because that was what everyone else seemed to be doing. A man wearing a red velvet jacket smiled down at me as I approached.

"Splendid, isn't it?"

"It's... uh –" I peered into the case at what looked like a weirdly shaped brick "– it's quite something."

"Are you interested in mineralogy? You must be, being the professor's daughter."

"Oh yes. Yes, it's all very..."

I hesitated, not because I was stuck in a big fat lie, but because I started feeling ... odd. That same feeling I'd gotten last time in the museum on the school trip: as though all the blood running through my body was growing hot. The scar on my left palm began to tingle.

Uh-oh.

"Excuse me," I said quickly, shoving my elderflower glass into his hand and backing away from the cabinet. "I need to get some air."

I turned and began pushing my way through the guests, aiming for the main entrance. I felt stronger this time round, as though I might be able to stop my powers blasting from my hands, but I didn't want to risk losing control. I glanced down at my hand and panicked as I saw a dim glow beginning to appear, like a flickering bulb. Why did this keep happening?

Just as I broke free from the main crowd, Dad grabbed my arm.

"Aurora, there you are. You forgot to come say hi when you arrived," he said, leaning down to give me a hug. "You look very pretty! Everything OK?"

I thought about telling him the truth but I knew that, after what happened last time in the museum, he'd suddenly panic and I didn't want him to worry when he already had so much to think about. I quickly put my hand behind my back.

"Everything's great," I said. "Well done, Dad, this is a great launch."

"I'm a bit nervous about my speech," he admitted quietly, fiddling with his shirt collar. "I've tried to make it short and sweet."

"Great. Perfect. Well, I'll leave you to go practice."

"Aurora —" he stopped me, looking about

us nervously "– you, um, haven't seen your mother anywhere, have you?"

"No, but she'll be here somewhere. Why?"

"Just . . . well. . . She's always been very good at making me feel relaxed and more confident. I was hoping she'd come tonight and I thought I saw her across the room earlier but I . . . well, I guess I was wrong because I haven't seen her for a while. Maybe it was a hallucination. Wishful thinking or something." He gave me a sad smile. "Well, I had better get back to my guests."

"Dad," I said hurriedly, still trying to push aside that warm, fluttering feeling in my stomach that was beginning to spread up my chest and down my arms, "she's really proud of you. Mum, I mean. There's no way she'd miss this. She'll be here in time for your speech."

He nodded and gave me another quick

hug before throwing his shoulders back and striding into the crowd. I darted between the mingling guests and rushed through the doorway and into the cold night air, inhaling deeply and instantly feeling better. I looked back over my shoulder suspiciously at the museum, wondering why on earth it had such a strange effect on me. I leaned against the wall, waiting for the glowing on my palm to ebb away and enjoying a moment away from the bustling throng. My feet were rubbing in my shoes, so I shook them off and slid on my sneakers. My dress was just about long enough for me to get away with it, as long as no one decided to study my footwear. Not that anyone was paying any attention to me.

I must have been a bit dizzier than I'd first thought because I kept hearing Kizzy's voice in the background. I shook my head and decided that I should go and get some water, pronto;

I shouldn't have given away that elderflower drink. I closed my eyes and took a couple of deep breaths, but there it was again: Kizzy's voice ringing through the air.

"Aurora! Aurora!"

Did I bang my head on the ostrich skeleton or something in my mad rush to get out of the museum just now?

"Aurora!"

I thought I'd been very clearheaded after I'd spoken to Dad; I'm sure I'd remember if I'd walked into anything.

"Aurora!"

Maybe I depend on Kizzy so much that her voice is now forever in my subconscious?

"AURORA BEAM, WOULD YOU LOOK OVER HERE!"

I jumped as I heard the shout from the line of guests up against the barriers leading to the entrance. Trying to push their way through the security guards at the front of the line were Kizzy, Georgie, Suzie and Fred, all waving madly at me.

"What are you doing here?" I asked, once I'd raced over to them and the security guards had allowed them to come through.

"We've been calling you!"

"No phones allowed," I explained, nodding at the security guards collecting phones from guests going in.

"Nice shoes," Georgie said, and winked, spotting the glitter peeking out at the bottom of my dress.

"What is wrong with your hearing?" Suzie huffed. "We could see you standing over there talking to yourself for ages."

"If you'd all wanted invitations to the event, you could have just asked." I shrugged. "I didn't think you'd want to come, but I'm sure if I just say to my dad—"

"That's not why we're here," Georgie said with a serious expression.

"We need you to see something," Fred said, sliding the strap of his heavy-looking gym bag off his shoulder and down to the ground.

"Can't it wait until tomorrow?" I laughed. "I'm loving your enthusiasm for this superhero club but this evening is kind of a big deal for my dad and I need to—"

"It can't wait," Kizzy said firmly, her tone taking me by surprise.

She leaned down and unzipped Fred's gym bag, pulling out a file and opening it to show me the old newspaper clipping inside, with a headline that read: *BLACKOUT BURGLAR CAUGHT RED-HANDED.*

"Twenty years ago, your mum stopped a major robbery. This guy, known as the Blackout Burglar, was a renowned criminal, capable of shutting down electrics and causing blackouts, giving him the perfect cover of darkness to steal anything he wanted."

"Yeah, I've heard of him," I said, vaguely remembering one of Mum's stories.

"He robbed houses, banks, anywhere you can think of with anything valuable," Georgie said, as Kizzy nodded, "but his specialty was jewelry, gems and precious stones."

"It was years before he was caught, but in the end, according to her notes, your mum was able to work out his next move," Suzie continued. "She waited until he caused a blackout on a glamorous

THE SENTINEL

BLACKOUT BURGLAR CAUGHT RED-HANDED

evening in London when a priceless diamond tiara went up for auction, then she used her powers to light the room." She sighed. "The tiara, by the way, was *so* gorgeous. Does your mum have access to that kind of thing or does it all go into evidence?"

"He was so shocked by the sudden flash of light," Fred continued, shooting Suzie an impatient look, "that your mum was able to pin him down and tie him up ready for the police to arrive. When she lit up the room, the hidden cameras she had placed earlier caught him red-handed. Perfect evidence to put him straight in jail."

"OK, this all sounds very cool," I said, "but what has some tiara burglar from twenty years ago got to do with right now?"

"Because the Blackout Burglar swore vengeance on your mum. It's reported in the article that he kept saying he would one day take his revenge on the 'light-beam woman.' The police just thought he was speaking rubbish to try and plead insanity. But he didn't, he pleaded guilty and was released from prison a few years later for good behavior."

"And?"

"Didn't you hear us?" Fred sighed in exasperation. "His specialty is diamonds and *precious stones*. Tonight is all about the most interesting precious stone discovery ever and, not only that, but your mum, his great nemesis, is married to the professor putting on the display. He knows who she is. It's the perfect revenge!"

"Wait a second, you think that—"

"Aurora," Kizzy said, tapping her finger at the newspaper clipping. "The photo."

I sighed and looked at the picture in the middle of the article of a young man being dragged away in handcuffs.

"What about it?"

"Look closer," Kizzy instructed. "Don't you recognize him?"

I brought the article closer and scrutinized the photograph. Suddenly, my breath caught in my throat and a feeling of ice-cold dread swept through my entire body. I brought my eyes up to meet Kizzy's.

"Mr. Mercury."

My head was spinning. It seemed impossible. Mr. Mercury, the most boring science teacher on the planet with a big bald head and coffee stains splattered across his shirts, was a world-class criminal? The Blackout Burglar?

It just didn't make any sense!

And yet...

The more I thought about it, the more it kind of did. He had always been weirdly interested in my dad's exhibition and the precious stones at the center of it. As soon as he'd arrived as a new teacher at the beginning of the year, he'd asked me about Dad's work and organizing a school trip to the museum.

"We think he used the school trip to scout out behind the scenes of the museum," Kizzy said, as the others nodded in agreement. "It was the perfect opportunity to do a reccy."

"A *reccy*? What's that?"

"When you check out the area ready for attack. He knows exactly where everything is and what to do when it comes to stealing the precious stones."

"I can't believe this," I whispered, shaking my head and still gripping the newspaper article. "You really think Mr. Mercury is going to steal from an exhibition?"

"Why else would he have wangled an invitation to this evening?" Georgie shrugged. "And you saw him on the trip, asking your dad hundreds of questions."

"Yeah, I mean, come on," Suzie said. "No one is *that* interested in a bunch of rocks."

"Precious stones," Kizzy corrected.

"Whatever, it's still lame, if you want my opinion," Suzie grumbled. "Why not rob somewhere like Tiffany's and take all the diamonds?"

"Diamonds," I repeated, as it all began to dawn on me. "The Dream Diamond."

"What dream diamond?"

"My aunt, she has this diamond. It's really precious. He saw her wearing it the other day when she came to pick me up and he knew what it was. He knew it was the Dream Diamond. He said so as soon as he saw it. He looked ... excited. I thought they were just flirting."

"Your aunt and Mr. Mercury were flirting?" Suzie wrinkled her nose. "Ew."

"It would make sense that he'd be able to identify things like that," Kizzy reasoned.

"Kizzy, he asked if she'd be wearing it tonight. I didn't even think about it at the time, but that's kind of a weird question to ask someone, right?"

"It's a double heist!" Fred cried excitedly. "He's going to take both!"

"How did Mum not recognize him at the parents' evening?" I asked, my eyebrows knitted in confusion.

"It's a pretty good disguise he's got going on," Georgie said. "And it's been a good few years; think how many criminals your mum puts away. She can't remember them all. Plus, you know," she shifted awkwardly, "your mum was probably a bit distracted with that fabulous ostrich running around and your aunt being there in a big ball gown. She didn't even realize her hair was a big ice block. It's understandable that she might not have noticed Mr. Mercury all that much."

"Seriously, though, who has an ostrich for a pet?" Suzie asked.

"He's very well accessorized," Georgie pointed out.

"Let's stay focused here," Kizzy said sternly. "Aurora, we think Mr. Mercury is going to try and steal the precious stones tonight and we have to stop him."

Fred lifted his gym bag up and patted it. "We brought plenty of supplies to bring down a bad guy."

"Yeah, because whoopee cushions are *super* helpful," Suzie muttered under her breath.

"Oh, and a bunch of colorful ribbons are really going to save the day," Fred retorted. "Good idea, Suzie; let's stop a big heist with bows in our hair."

"It's not hair ribbon, pea brain," she snarled. "It's rhythmic gymnastics ribbon. And I've won four competitions with those."

"The point is," Georgie said over them loudly, "that we're ready to help."

"But I haven't seen Mr. Mercury all night," I replied hopefully. "Maybe he got cold feet."

"No way," Fred snorted. "He's been waiting for this moment for a long time. Everyone loves a good revenge and this is his time. I reckon he got the job at the school *specifically* because he found out that Professor Beam's children went there. A school trip is the perfect cover to get all the information you need about a place without arousing any suspicion. It's classic comic book stuff."

"Aurora, does Mr. Mercury know about your superpowers?" Georgie asked.

I shook my head. "I don't think so."

"Then we have an advantage," Fred nodded, his eyes twinkling. "He won't be expecting you to get in his way."

"But he knows your mum will. We need

to find her and tell her," Kizzy said, glancing toward the entrance. "And we need to tell her now. He could strike at any minute."

"You're right." I nodded, squeezing her hand. "She should be here by now. Let's go."

I hurried toward the door with the superhero club hot on my heels, hit by an overwhelming surge of determination. The shock and fear I'd felt a few moments ago on discovering my science teacher was in fact a criminal mastermind was replaced by the resolution to stop him in his tracks. There was no way I was going to let Mr. Mercury get away with this.

I was glad I was wearing my special Lightning Girl sneakers. They made me feel confident somehow.

As soon as I stepped back into the main gallery, the scar on my palm started to tingle. I clenched my fists. I didn't have time for any of that. A security woman on the door immediately stopped us to take the others' phones and check their bags. Her forehead furrowed in confusion as she peered into Fred's gym bag.

"Is that ... an ant farm?"

"Yes," he admitted, looking at it lovingly. "You know how it is, you can't leave the children at home alone."

She blinked at him, completely stunned, and for a moment I thought she was going to kick him out, but she finally gave him a wary smile and pointed him in the direction of the cloakroom in case he wanted to leave it in there.

"If you would like, I'm sure the attendant will take good care of your ... ants. And all those whoopee cushions," she added.

Fred thanked her and we approached the crowd, standing on our tiptoes, trying to spot Mum among the loudly chattering guests.

"Anyone see her?" Georgie asked, her eyes

darting across the room.

"It's jammed in here," Suzie grumbled as someone knocked her shoulder going past. "As if a few pebbles can draw this kind of a crowd."

"*Precious stones*, not pebbles," Kizzy corrected before turning to me. "I can't see her anywhere."

"Me neither."

"Maybe your aunt will know where she is," Georgie suggested. "Isn't that her ostrich? His monocle is so on point."

She pointed toward the far side of the room where I saw that Alfred had discovered a fun new game. Standing perfectly still like a statue, as though he was part of a taxidermy display, he was waiting for guests to come up and inspect him and then suddenly lunging at them, making them scream in terror. As an unsuspecting female guest became his next victim, screeching at the top of her lungs as he came to life, I saw Dad excuse himself from a nearby conversation with a pained expression and attempt to tell Alfred off, but Alfred just wiggled his bum feathers in Dad's face defiantly and stalked off to help himself to an entire tray of canapés.

"I can't see Aunt Lucinda though. And trust me, in the dress she's wearing, you can't miss her."

We continued to desperately search the crowd until someone tapped my shoulder. I spun round hoping it might be Mum but it was only Alexis and Clara.

"Dad's speech is about to start," Clara informed me, her book tucked under her arm.

"How are you feeling?" Alexis raised his eyebrows, looking me up and down. "You don't look ill to me."

"What are you talking about? I'm feeling fine. Have you seen Mum?"

"Yeah."

"Great! Where is she?" I asked, gripping his arm.

"You tell me," he said, shaking me off and giving me a weird look. "She was with you."

"No, she wasn't," I said, as the others

gathered round me.

"How come you were allowed to bring friends?" Alexis grumbled, crossing his arms. "And did you guys not get the black tie memo?"

"Alexis, it's really important that you tell me where Mum is."

"I already told you, I don't know. She was with you. And Mr. Mercury."

I felt Kizzy gasp at my shoulder.

"What do you mean?" I squeaked. "Mr. Mercury was here? With Mum?"

"OK, I don't know what is going on," Alexis sighed, holding up his hands. "All I know is Mum was standing here with me a while ago, complaining about feeling dizzy, and then Mr. Mercury came out of nowhere and told her that you were really ill. He took her to go help you out. I thought it was probably the crab cakes, they smell really weird."

"Aunt Lucinda must have had one of those

too, then," Clara shrugged. "She felt odd and Mr. Mercury offered to escort her to get some water."

"Where did they go?" I practically yelled, causing Alexis to look at me, completely taken aback.

"Whoa! I don't know, they just disappeared into the crowd. Don't worry though, they'll be back in time for Dad's speech."

I turned around to huddle with the others.

"This is *not* good," I hissed. "What do we do?"

"He'll have wanted them out of the way," Kizzy replied, as we all nodded vigorously. "Does your Aunt Lucinda have superpowers as well?"

"Yes. I don't know if he knows that too."

"He's smart enough not to risk it." Kizzy looked thoughtful. "Where would he take them? He can't have gotten far, not if he plans on stealing the precious stones tonight."

"We should tell your dad," Georgie suggested. "He needs to get the stones out of here."

"Georgie's right, the stones are at their most vulnerable when they're out on display," Kizzy agreed. "Then we go rescue your mum."

"But he can't take the rocks in front of all these people," Suzie pointed out. "There would be a load of witnesses; he'd be silly to try it with everyone here surrounding them. He'd be stopped by those hot, muscly security guys as soon as he stepped past the rope."

"Not if they couldn't see him," Fred pointed out. "He's the Blackout Burglar, remember?"

"We don't have much time." Georgie nodded toward my dad, who was tweaking his bow tie and glancing for the last time at his notes. "We have to go tell him now to move them."

We broke apart and had just begun to make

our way through the bustling mass of people to get to Dad when there was a loud bang and the entire museum was plunged into total darkness.

Were we too late?

17

It all happened very quickly.

As the room went pitch-black, there was a ripple of gasps across the crowd. My dad immediately called out for everyone to remain calm, but I could hear the sense of confusion and worry in his tone as he tried to work out what was going on. Kizzy felt for my arm in the darkness.

"He's here," she whispered fearfully.

I heard the sound of Fred's bag being unzipped behind me and the rustle of him scrambling around in it, grabbing what he could.

"We're going to fix this as soon as possible," my dad called out as the whispers of the guests began to grow more panicked. "There must be a fault with the electricity. Try not to move, we don't want any injuries!"

Suddenly there was a loud crash of glass and everyone began screaming. It was complete chaos.

"The gems!" I heard Georgie gasp.

"Why did they take our phones?" Suzie wailed. "We could have used the flashlight."

"We don't need phones," Kizzy replied in the darkness. "We have a much brighter light. Aurora, quick! Before he gets away."

"I can't! Everyone will see!"

"We don't have any other option!" Kizzy insisted. "Aurora, your mum and aunt may be in trouble. We need to stop Mr. Mercury; we can't let him get away with this. You can do it, Aurora!"

As much as I didn't want to admit it to myself, Kizzy was right. I had to stop him, even if it meant revealing the secret I'd promised Mum I'd keep. Everything would change after this. But I didn't have time to think about consequences.

Even though it was already dark, I closed my eyes, shutting out the chatter of confusion around me and remembering everything Mum had taught me in those training sessions. My family needed me and no one else was here to save them. I had to do this.

My superpowers came easily.

I don't know if it was because I knew how important it was to get it right, or if it was something to do with this place, but I'd never felt so powerful. My hands were already tingling and so I simply stopped concentrating on hiding the glow. I embraced the warmth spreading through my blood and the feeling

became so strong, it was as though I could see it shimmering underneath my skin. Beams shot from my palms and the entire gallery was suddenly bathed in the shimmering radiance of bright sparkling light.

It was different from the last incident in the museum because I was completely in control. It took all my concentration to make sure that the surge of energy emanating from me was contained and no one would be knocked back by the force. Instead, it was as though the extraordinary feeling of magical warmth that tingled in my hands, and spread through my body every time I commanded my powers, was being transferred to all those around me. I could see it in their faces as they lowered their hands in amazement, having shielded their eyes from the first burst of light. They were feeling it too.

"Wow," Suzie whispered, watching me with

awe. "This whole glowing look really suits you."

"You did it!" Kizzy squealed. "She did it! Go, Lightning Girl!"

It wasn't until that moment, that the whole "Lightning Girl" thing really hit me. I guess up until then, it was simply a name that my friends had randomly come up with and I hadn't given all that much thought to. But, when Kizzy cried it out at the top of her lungs in front of a crowd of people who were depending on me to help them, it felt like more than just a name. I don't know, it felt like my *destiny* or something, like I was supposed to play this part.

And it felt BRILLIANT.

Out of the corner of my eye I saw Clara staring up at me in wonder and Alexis frozen to the spot, his mouth hanging wide open. Suddenly Georgie pointed across the sea of guests whose eyes were glued to me in stunned silence.

"There he is! Mr. Mercury!"

For a split second, Mr. Mercury froze in panic, but then his eyes narrowed with determination and he furiously lurched forward, barging his way toward the exit, knocking guests mercilessly to the floor as he went, sending canapés and champagne glasses scattering.

"We have to stop him!" Fred yelled. "Georgie, here!"

Georgie had already begun racing ahead to get in Mr. Mercury's path. Fred reached into his bag and, without hesitation, threw a can of hair spray high up into the air. She caught it with ease and ripped off the lid just in time. As Mr. Mercury barreled past, she held out the can and sprayed it in his face with all her might. He shrieked in pain as the hair spray stung his eyes, momentarily bringing him to a halt.

He cried out angrily and pushed Georgie aside, sending her stumbling backward into a group of guests who caught her.

"Out of my way!" Mr. Mercury roared, his eyes now red and puffy and streaming with tears.

He darted toward the door, but while Georgie had been attacking him with hair spray, Suzie had rushed ahead and she now sprang into action. Poised perfectly with her arms stretched up in the air, she bent her knees gracefully and leapt upward, her knees tucking up and flying up into the air backward over her head, her feet connecting with the center of Mr. Mercury's chest, and knocking him to the floor as she landed. It was the best backward somersault she had ever done.

"Bummer," she said crossly, as she regained her balance after a slight stumble. "I'd have lost points on that landing."

"YES!" Georgie gleefully cried. "TEN POINTS!"

Mr. Mercury scrambled to his feet with a face like thunder and instantly lunged straight for Suzie, who quickly edged

away from his explosive roar. But she needn't have worried because Fred was already right behind him and, before Mr. Mercury could

take another step forward, Fred pulled the waistband of Mr. Mercury's trousers back and poured in the entire ant farm. A plume of dust puffed up into the air as his waistband pinged back, closing in the mound of sand and its inhabitants. Unsure of exactly what it was that Fred had shoved down his trousers, Mr. Mercury's alarmed expression changed into a mocking smirk as he reached down his waistband and let a handful of sand seep through his fingers.

"You think a bit of sand and dirt is going to stop me?" Mr. Mercury growled, towering threateningly over his student. "I'm disappointed in you, Fred."

"I think you'll be a little more disappointed when I tell you that I ended up going against the advice you gave me at the beginning of term. You know, when I asked you what ants

I should use for my ant farm?" Fred grinned back at him triumphantly. "As soon as you told me to avoid red ants because they can bite, I knew they were the ones for me."

Mr. Mercury's smile froze as Fred's meaning dawned on him.

"Apparently, they only sting in self-defense, so, whatever you do, don't try and harm them because there are *loads* of them in your pants right now."

Mr. Mercury cried out and began hopping up and down on the spot, wriggling around, twitching and flinging his legs out one at a time, as though he were attempting

some kind of jig. Fred burst into infectious hysterics and I couldn't help but crack a smile as Mr. Mercury squirmed and twisted, crying out, "Ooooooooh, aaaaaaaaaah, ooooooooooh!"

He quickly undid his belt and let his trousers drop to the floor, eagerly kicking them off into a pile, leaving him standing there in his socks, shoes and bright-green underpants with little ducks all over them.

The security guards had by now gotten over the fact that there was a human light bulb in the middle of the room, and had raced over to help us, blocking Mr. Mercury's exit.

"Stay away from me!" he barked, sweat pouring down his face. "I'm warning you!"

His eyes quickly scanned the room for an idea as security slowly approached him. Spotting a fire escape to his right, tucked behind some of the exhibition cabinets, he sprinted at full pelt toward it, dodging some brave guests' outstretched arms as they attempted and failed to stop him.

I stopped breathing as I realized that he was going to get away.

The light from my hands began to ebb and dim as I lost concentration. I desperately cried out for him to stop. It had all been for nothing.

But just as he stretched outward to push through the fire escape, a blurred object swept suddenly in front of him.

There was a loud thud as he collided with Alfred at speed, before stumbling backward dizzily, falling and landing sprawled out on the floor like a starfish.

"Go, Alfred!" I cried gleefully as the ostrich ruffled his feathers indignantly.

Considering he doesn't like anyone except Aunt Lucinda touching him at the best of times, I can't imagine the ostrich was all that pleased about a strange man hitting him square on in the chest. He didn't seem too put out though and, after shooting an irritated glare at the whimpering Mr. Mercury lying on the floor, sauntered off to eye up a display of Roman coins. I'm still not sure if he meant to stop Mr. Mercury or not, but I will never speak ill of Alfred again. No matter how many items of my clothing he destroys.

The room exploded with cheers and exalted whoops as the security guards rushed over to pin Mr. Mercury down and get his hands behind his back, ensuring there was no chance of his escape. As they lugged him to his feet still in a daze, Kizzy reached toward the small pouch tied with black string round his neck, and held it upside down, tipping the precious stones into her hand. Among them was the Dream Diamond. She held them up in the air victoriously, prompting rapturous applause from the guests.

"Yes!" Fred cried, punching the air. "Go, Burglar Busting Gang!"

Suzie and Georgie both looked at him in disgust.

"Burglar Busting Gang?" Suzie sighed. "Really?"

"Fine. The name needs work." He grinned at her. "Still. We were awesome."

Now that Mr. Mercury had been safely captured, the attention of the room returned to me. Exhausted from having to sustain the light beams all this time, I let my hands drop, stopping my powers and causing the room to fall back into darkness, except for my left palm which continued to glow. There was an eruption of whispers as I crouched on the ground, feeling completely drained. Dad was suddenly at my side, his arm around me.

"Aurora," he whispered, his eyes full of grateful tears.

"Dad. I'm fine. You need to find Mum."

"What do you mean?"

"Mr. Mercury tricked her and Aunt Lucinda. They're somewhere in the museum."

His eyes widened in horror, but then he got this determined look on his face and turned to instruct Alexis and Clara to stay with me.

"Where are you going?" Clara asked.

He puffed out his chest and straightened his bow tie.

"I'm going to rescue my wife," he said in this gruff, heroic voice as though he was in a Bond movie.

If I wasn't so worried about Mum, it would have been hilarious.

"How will you be able to see where you're going? The whole of the museum's electricity has cut out," Clara pointed out, glancing at the security guards who had now sourced some phones and were turning on the flashlights.

"How will you be able to find her?"

"I know this museum like the back of my hand. Trust me," he said proudly, "there's no one better for the job."

Alexis appeared unable to say anything and was still staring at me in complete shock. He hadn't blinked for about five minutes.

"So," Clara said, crouching in front of me, her face lighting up in the small but still distinct glow of my scar, "is it just me, or is there something you need to tell us?"

18

"It was an explosion of light. Like lightning! It came right out of her hands. *Her hands...*"

"There were, like, sparks and beams and she was, like, *glowing*. I thought I'd had one too many glasses of champagne, but everyone else here saw it too..."

"At first I was a bit scared because a human shouldn't be able to do stuff like that, you know? But she seems like a nice young girl. As for that ostrich..."

"I've never seen anything like it. It was

simply magical. And the light ... it was the most dazzling thing I've ever seen. Something about it made me feel comforted. It made me feel happy..."

"I think I heard someone call her Light Girl, or Lightning Girl, maybe, but I still feel as though I'm in a state of shock, so I may have misheard..."

"It was WEIRD. What is she? An alien?"

I sighed as we continued to overhear snippets of the various police interviews going on around us.

"Why do people automatically assume I'm an alien?" I asked Kizzy, who was sitting next to me. "Why isn't the first assumption that I have superpowers? Or growing pains? That's what I thought it was when it first happened."

Kizzy snorted. "You thought sparks flying from your fingertips were *growing pains*?"

"It makes more sense than being an alien," I said defensively.

We hadn't moved from the spot where I'd sat down in the middle of the gallery, except now the lights were back on, thanks to an electrician that the police squad had helpfully brought along with them. I was still feeling a bit strange, even though some time had passed, and the scar on my palm was still glowing. Mum insisted that I stay put for a bit longer, despite probably being in the way of the police and the forensic team and stuff.

Mum should really have been the one relaxing considering she'd been stuck in a vault this whole time. Mr. Mercury had led her and Aunt Lucinda down to the mineralogy storeroom and locked them in one of the large vaults at the back. It had been the first place Dad had looked when he'd raced off to find them.

"I remembered that on the school trip Mr. Mercury had asked me a few odd questions. One of them was how big the vaults were that I keep my future displays in," Dad had explained when we'd all been reunited. "I told him that they varied, but some of them were big enough for me to be able to sit in quite easily."

"Wow, Dad," I had smiled. "Quick thinking."

"You really were amazing," Mum had gushed, making him blush ferociously.

"It's nothing," he had mumbled, embarrassed. "Nice for *you* to be rescued for once."

Now they were standing nearby with Aunt Lucinda, talking in hushed voices as the police continued to investigate the crime scene around us. Georgie, Kizzy, Suzie and Fred had all given their version of events – "frankly, my red ants are the real heroes here today" – and were now sitting in a circle with me on the floor.

I watched Mum talking animatedly to Dad, who was clutching the box containing the precious stones and nodding slowly, and Aunt Lucinda interrupting every now and then with dramatic "ooh"s and "aah"s. Earlier, Mum had admitted to me quietly that the real torture of being locked in the vault was that her twin sister was shut in with her. Apparently the ruffles on Lucinda's dress took up most of the space and at one point she insisted on singing songs from musicals to lift their spirits.

The three of them nodded together and then they wandered over to us.

"Aurora," Mum began, "can we have a word?"

I got to my feet a little shakily, as that tingling feeling continued to buzz under my skin, and, under the curious eyes of the superhero club and my siblings, I followed

Mum, Dad and Aunt Lucinda to a quieter part of the gallery, away from all the police and guests still being questioned.

"What's going on?"

"Your Aunt Lucinda and I had a lot of time to talk when we were shut in that vault together. And, well, something came to our attention." Mum hesitated. "Your palm..."

"I don't know why it's still glowing," I said, clutching my fist tightly to stop it being so obvious.

"We think we know why."

"What's going on?" I asked, scanning their faces for any giveaways.

"The incident on the school trip, when you couldn't control your powers. Well, it turns out, I feel a bit weird here in the museum too. And Lucinda does as well."

"I can't believe I didn't notice this whole time," Dad said, shaking his head in bafflement.

"Notice what?"

Mum nodded at him and he held out the box, carefully lifting the lid to show the stones sitting comfortably in a silk setting.

"Did you get a good look at the precious stones?" Dad asked me carefully.

"Are you serious?" I sighed. "After everything that's happened, you want to quiz me about the exhibition? No offense, Dad, I'm sure the ancient stones are very nice, but we have a lot more to discuss."

"He's not quizzing you on them," Mum said gently. "Look closely at this one."

I peered down at the smooth stone she was pointing to, the one in the middle of the box. It was one of the bigger stones in the collection, just smaller than my palm, and you could slightly make out a swirled pattern in its middle.

"That's…" I snapped my head up so that my eyes locked with Mum's. "That's the same pattern as my scar!"

I held out my palm and the glowing intensified. Dad shut the lid of the box with a sigh.

"I've studied these precious stones for months; I've written papers on them; I organized an entire exhibition all about them. And I failed to notice that one of them had the same swirl as the scar on my daughter's palm."

"How were you to know that they were linked?" Mum said, stroking his arm comfortingly. "It's not that uncommon a pattern or a particularly obvious symbol."

"Wait a second, my palm is glowing because of . . . that pebble?"

"Precious stone," Dad corrected, looking pained.

"I tried to tell you the day we stole that diamond together—" Aunt Lucinda began nonchalantly.

"You mean the day *you* stole that diamond. I was tricked. And you said nothing about a pebble."

"*Precious stones.*"

"Sorry, Dad. Precious stones."

"I tried to explain the part of the legend that your mother neglected to tell you," said Aunt Lucinda sniffily.

"I did try to tell her," Mum insisted. "When we first found out she had powers, I wanted to tell her the full story, but Henry wouldn't let me because he didn't want to overwhelm her."

"Well, now hang on," Dad said defensively, "you never told me it was factual. You told me that it was just legend, passed on from generation to generation. In fact, I distinctly remember you saying to me years ago that you thought that part of the story was laughable. So, it didn't seem necessary to tell her."

"Tell me WHAT?" I asked in exasperation.

Mum took a deep breath. "In the story about how our family were first given powers, Dawn went to the aurora borealis to restore light to the world. Well, I never told you how *exactly* she got that power."

"The Light of the World," Aunt Lucinda said, gesturing to the box in my Dad's hands. "That stone. According to the myth, she discovered the stone and as she took it in her hand, light was restored to the world."

"That stone? That *exact* stone?" I blinked at Mum. "Are you *sure*?"

"It makes sense as to why all of our powers were suddenly heightened around it when we were in the museum; why you lost control being near it last time; why your powers showed themselves so early when it was discovered and brought to this country; and how you managed such an extraordinary light today." Mum smiled warmly. "I hear it was magnificent."

"If it is that specific stone, then its discovery has made us particularly vulnerable," Aunt Lucinda huffed. "If it gets into the wrong hands..."

"What? What would happen?"

"Technically, if it is what we think it is, then it's the source of all our power," Mum explained gently. "If it was destroyed, we'd most certainly lose the superpowers we have."

"Which is why it should be in my possession, safe and sound," Aunt Lucinda insisted. "Honestly, Kiyana, you have enough on your plate."

"There is no chance you are walking away with that stone, Lucinda," Mum said firmly, "so you might as well give up trying to persuade me otherwise."

Aunt Lucinda inhaled deeply. "Just because you're a few minutes older than me, doesn't mean you know best."

"Actually, that's exactly what it means."

"All right, no more squabbling," Dad said. "Until we work out what we're going to do, the stone will be kept safe."

"You should at least tell me where you're going to put it; I have a right to know," Aunt

Lucinda grumbled.

"Is that why Mr. Mercury was trying to steal it? He knew about this?"

Mum shook her head. "From what I gather, he's insisting he was working for someone else. Apparently, someone approached him and offered him the chance to get back at me for putting him in jail all those years ago and told him that he'd get some precious stones out of it. According to his statement, if he pulled off this job then he could take all of them, bar one."

"And you can guess which one that was," Dad added.

"Mr. Mercury was just a puppet in all this? There's someone else who planned it?"

"Something like that." Mum sighed. "But he's refusing to say on whose orders he was acting."

"The police will get it out of him," Dad said reassuringly. "He's hardly one to show loyalty."

"So, someone out there knows the value of that stone, you think?" I asked.

Mum and Dad shared a look.

"We're not sure. But I'm going to find out," Mum answered determinedly.

"Well, darlings, it's been a blast, but I'm afraid I'm done with this particular episode," Aunt Lucinda announced, clapping her hands for Alfred to come over from the sofa on which he was reclined, using his beak to flick through one of the museum's exhibition brochures. "If you'll just hand over my diamond, then I'll get going."

"What diamond?"

"Don't joke with me, Kiyana, I simply don't have time for any more nonsense. I'm already late for my flight to Bora Bora and you know how Alfred hates to rush through duty free."

"The Dream Diamond is going back to the auction house you stole it from all those years ago. I already contacted them to let them know it had been safely found."

Aunt Lucinda pursed her lips. "You do know how to annoy me, Kiyana."

"What are sisters for?"

A smile crept across Aunt Lucinda's face.

"Well, then, I'll simply have to start making new plans to steal it back. I do love a challenge. Aurora," she put a hand on my shoulder, "I'll be keeping an eye on you from afar. Those powers are too strong to be wasted on 'the greater good.'"

She pinched my cheek and then swept away through the museum toward the exit, with Alfred trotting happily next to her.

"Toodle-loo, darlings!" she said, disappearing through the door without looking back.

"I have a terrible feeling that we might be seeing them both sooner than we hope," Dad said, making Mum laugh. She threw her arm around my shoulders and led me back toward my friends.

"I'm so proud of you, Aurora. You were amazing, a real superhero." She kissed me on the head.

"No way, the others did most of the work."

"There's something special about you, Aurora, and I can't put my finger on it. You have a warmth in your powers, something unique. I think that might be your extra perk, you know," she said quietly before we reached the rest of the group. She stopped me and turned to face me straight on. "And your scar is the pattern on that stone. That means something."

I traced the raised swirl on my palm. "Do you think that's a bad thing?"

"I'm not sure. But whatever it means, we'll work it out. Together."

"Thanks, Mum. And I'm sorry that everyone knows about the superpowers now. Everyone here saw it. They think I'm an alien."

"Don't worry about that," she chuckled. "For now, I reckon we all deserve the rest of the night off."

"I agree," Dad said, raising his voice as we came to stand next to the others who were still sitting cross-legged in their circle. "How about everyone comes to ours for a hot chocolate?"

"Sounds good!" Kizzy grinned, standing up. "I'm in."

"Us too," Georgie added, with Suzie and Fred nodding in agreement.

"And ... Mum too?" Clara said hopefully, coming over to take her hand.

Mum lifted her eyes to meet Dad's, waiting for his answer. He beamed down at her.

"Mum too," he said softly.

Clara threw her arms round Mum's waist, while I helped Alexis to his feet. I think he was still thrown by the whole superpower thing because I kept catching him giving me these strange looks, as though he was trying to work it all out in his head.

"I'm still just me, you know," I said, nudging him with my elbow as the others made their way to the exit.

"I guess," he said, before adding, "maybe a little cooler. And, hey, if you superheroes ever need to hack into any computer systems to save the day, you know where to come."

He even let me give him a hug for at least two seconds before batting me away and walking ahead to catch up with Mum, Dad and Clara. I fell into step with my friends.

"Excellent aim with the hair spray, Georgie," Fred was saying. "He didn't know what hit him."

"Thanks for throwing it to me, that was good thinking. You shoving all those ants down his trousers was brilliant."

"Yes," Suzie said, as we walked out into

the cold air and flashing blue lights of all the police cars, "I agree. Literally ants in his pants. Inspired."

"What about your backflip? BOOF! Right in his chest, knocked him clean to the floor! Your aim was perfect."

"And Kizzy, working this all out in the first place." Georgie smiled, making Kizzy blush. "If you hadn't discovered what Mr. Mercury was up to, he would have gotten away with everything."

"I've been thinking about a name for the superhero club and I think I've got a good one," Fred announced, prompting a collective groan. "Hey! You haven't even heard it yet!"

"Go on then," I said.

"It's inspired by you, Aurora, having just witnessed you doing your thing in there," he replied. "What do you guys think of ... the Bright Sparks."

Suzie and Georgie looked pleasantly surprised and Kizzy began slowly nodding.

"The Bright Sparks," she repeated. "I like it."

"Bright Sparks it is," Georgie said, punching Fred playfully on the arm. "Not bad, Fred."

"Defeating bad guys, coming up with awesome names, it's all in a day's work," he boasted, grinning.

When we got home, the others hurried into the warmth of the house, greeted by an ecstatic Kimmy.

I stood back for a moment in the hallway, watching them all head into the kitchen, chatting and laughing loudly. Kizzy was talking animatedly to Clara about a book they'd both read; Fred was teasing Suzie, trying to encourage Kimmy to jump up on her; and Dad

was filling Georgie in on the knack to making the perfect hot chocolate, while Alexis rolled his eyes and made faces behind Dad's back, making Georgie giggle.

"Are you all right, Aurora?" Mum asked, hanging back with me.

"I was just thinking about all of the crazy things that happened today, and everything that's gone on in the past few weeks and, I don't know –" I shrugged "– I'm just ... really happy."

"What did I tell you? Superpowers are pretty great."

"Maybe." I grinned, leaning into her as we both watched Dad waltz around the kitchen with Kimmy, making everyone burst into laughter. "But I wasn't talking about the superpowers."

ACKNOWLEDGEMENTS

A heartfelt and huge thank you to everyone at
Scholastic, it has been a dream! Lauren Fortune,
Aimee Stewart, Rachel Phillipps, Roisin O'Shea,
Penelope Daukes, Andrew Biscomb
and the whole team.

To Katy Birchall, thank you for making this creative
process super easy and so much fun, you are amazing.

To Lauren Gardner, you are more than an agent –
thank you for your brilliant ideas and enthusiasm for
Aurora and for making this happen! I owe you one :)

To James Lancett, thank you so much for bringing all
of my characters to life with your art. You did an
incredible job and I am over the moon.

A special thank you to Team Alesha: Malcolm Blair & Bernadette Francis.

To my love Azuka, thank you for your endless love and always believing in me.

To my mum, Beverley, thank you for teaching me about love, light, healing & precious stones.

And last but not least, to all the readers of this book, may you always carry love and compassion in your heart, believe in a higher power greater than yourself and never forget that you are the light and that you have all the super powers you will ever need inside yourself already!

HAPPY READING :)

SUPERHERO STATS

AURORA BEAM/LIGHTNING GIRL

★ **HEIGHT**: 4 ft. 11 inches

★ **KNOWN FOR:** Shooting beams of light from her hands

★ **COULDN'T LIVE WITHOUT**: Her dog, Kimmy

SUPERHERO STATS

KIZZY CARPENTER/THE BRAINS

⭐ **HEIGHT**: 4 ft. 9 inches

⭐ **KNOWN FOR**: Planning and researching

⭐ **COULDN'T LIVE WITHOUT**: Her encyclopedia

SUPERHERO STATS

FRED PEPE/PRESIDENT OF THE BRIGHT SPARKS

★ **HEIGHT**: 5 ft.

★ **KNOWN FOR:** Distracting the enemy – often with his ant far

★ **COULDN'T LIVE WITHOUT:** His whoopee cushion

SUPERHERO STATS

SUZIE BRAVO/FLEXI-GIRL

* **HEIGHT:** 4 ft. 11 inches

* **KNOWN FOR:** Her gymnastic skills

* **COULDN'T LIVE WITHOUT:** Her collection of medals and trophies

SUPERHERO STATS

GEORGIE TAYLOR/STYLIST

★ **HEIGHT:** 4 ft. 9 inches

★ **KNOWN FOR:** Always having a handy can of hair spray

★ **COULDN'T LIVE WITHOUT:** Designer sunglasses

KIMMY

* **HEIGHT**: 1 ft. 8 inches

* **KNOWN FOR:** Being the best dog ever

* **COULDN'T LIVE WITHOUT:** Veggie quiche (and Aurora)

THE WEEKL

END O
WORLD
– ALIEN
IN LO

In an amazing scoop, the *Weekly Herald* can confirm evidence of a hostile alien attack in a local garden. Mrs. Crow, neighbor to the Beam family whose garden was destroyed in this dramatic event, gave us her firsthand eyewitness account.

HE
MINENT
ATTACK
L GARDEN

en invasion! I saw it! I saw it!
flash of light in next door's
t was so powerful it nearly knocked
ur fence! Blew me right over onto my
n! Gerald! GERALD! TELL THE NICE
SPAPER MAN!" commented Mrs. Crow
ing our exclusive interview. As our
mpending doom approaches, the *Weekly
Herald* would like to remind our readers

that the local supermarket is offering
two for one on canned goods – stock
up your cupboards for the apocalypse.
Our exclusive peek over the fence into the
garden of the Beams showed wreckage,
scorched grass, and an upturned birdbath
– clearly the work of sinister forces.
The Beam family declined to comment.

UNBREAKABLE
PINKY PROMISE!

THE BRIGHT SPARKS
CODE OF CONDUCT

1. Keep Aurora's powers TOP SECRET.

2. No secrets between members of the Bright Sparks.

3. Never trust a science teacher.

4. Follow Georgie's fashion advice.

5. Keep Aurora's powers TOP SECRET!!

Photo by John Wright

ALESHA DIXON first found fame as part of Brit-nominated and Mobo Award-winning group Mis-teeq, which achieved 2 platinum albums and 7 top ten hits, before going on to become a platinum-selling solo artist in her own right. Alesha's appearance on *Strictly Come Dancing* in 2007 led to her winning the series and becoming a judge for three seasons.

Since then she has presented and hosted many UK TV shows including CBBC dance show *Alesha's Street Dance Stars*, *Children In Need*, *Sport Relief*, *Your Face Sounds Familiar* and ITV's *Dance, Dance, Dance*. She is a hugely popular judge on *Britain's Got Talent*.

"My inspiration to create a superhero called Lightning Girl began with wanting my young daughter to feel empowered. It's been a dream to create a strong role model that any child can look up to - I want my readers to see themselves in Aurora, who is dealing with trouble at home and trouble at school alongside her new powers.

I also have a love of precious stones and their healing properties; I have always been fascinated with their spectacular colors and the positive energy that they bring. As human beings we are always searching for something greater within ourselves and a deeper meaning to life and it's my belief that we all have a light within us that can affect change and bring good to the world... we just have to harness it! :)

Enter **AURORA BEAM!**"

Photo by Ian Arnold

Katy Birchall is the author of the side-splittingly funny *The It Girl: Superstar Geek*, *The It Girl: Team Awkward*, *The It Girl: Don't Tell the Bridesmaid* and *Secrets of a Teenage Heiress*.

Katy won the 24/7 Theater Festival Award for Most Promising New Comedy Writer with her very serious play about a ninja monkey at a dinner party.

Her pet Labradors are the loves of her life, she is mildly obsessed with Jane Austen and one day she hopes to wake up as an elf in *The Lord of the Rings*.

READ THEM ALL